BETRAYED VALOR

BETRAYED VALOR

THE UNKNOWN STORY OF THE HEROES
OF MISSION HALYARD

ANDA VRANJES

gatekeeper press

Published by Gatekeeper Press
3971 Hoover Rd. Suite 77
Columbus, OH 43123-2839

ISBN: 9781619844339
eISBN: 9781619844346

Printed in the United States of America

DEDICATION

THIS BOOK IS dedicated to my husband Ilija, daughter Aleksia, and son Dejan. Thank you for your support and for giving me the time and space to tell this story. Your encouragement means the world to me.

It is also dedicated to my parents, brother and niece, +Vlasto, Milka, Milos and Milijana. For my entire life, you have encouraged me to fulfill my dreams. Thank you for recognizing something in me that I didn't always see for myself.

Last, but definitely not least, this book is dedicated to the five hundred US Military Airmen shot down in Nazi Occupied Yugoslavia during WWII as well as to the Serbian Chetniks and US Military who rescued them. Their sacrifices for freedom and justice should never be forgotten.

CONTENTS

ACKNOWLEDGMENTS

THE MEN OF the Halyard Mission spent their lives sharing the story of their daring rescue with everyone who would take the time to listen. It was an amazing piece of US history that can soon be forgotten. For it to endure and gain its rightful place in history, we must do our part to share it.

When I started writing this book, I reached out and found the children of one of the men who took part in the rescue. One replied to my email immediately, acknowledging he was the son, however, he never responded to further inquiries. The daughter never responded.

Upon further research, I found a fantastic resource in the book, *The Forgotten 500* by Gregory Freeman. His book is an amazing non-fiction resource for anyone looking for information on the Halyard Mission (aka Operation Halyard) and I highly recommend it to everyone.

In addition, I found David Martin's *The Web of Disinformation* to be another amazing resource. His book not only references the Halyard Mission, but it also details the grave mistake Winston Churchill made in switching his support from Mihailovic to Tito. Again, another book I highly recommend.

However, even though I found the above two resources and

many online resources, I ran into brick walls in terms of finding additional primary sources.

One day I was at a dinner at my priest's house and my book came up in conversation. I shared that I wanted to write this book and that I wished I had access to additional sources. It was there that I found out that the family of Major Richard Felman, a rescued Airman who was relentless in sharing his story with the world, donated their father's memorabilia from the Halyard Mission and his life's work to the Church. I had been searching for primary resources all over the country and it was under my nose the whole time!

My priest gave me access to Major Felman's collection and I was like a kid in a candy shop. I spent hours with the material-file cabinets full of documents, letters to Congress, Congressional letters to Major Felman, cassette tapes interviews - you name it! I could not believe my fortune in having all of this information at my fingertips! And one of the greatest sources was the book *Mihailovic and I,* by Major Felman. It was his own personal account of his days stranded behind enemy lines and the rescue.

About a year into the project, time was getting the best of me and I was suffering from a major case of writer's block. One afternoon, I sat down at the computer to write and struggle. I remember vividly questioning my ability to write this book. I was on the verge of giving up the whole idea.

Staring at the computer, I decided to read my email instead. I noticed I had a message from someone unfamiliar. I normally just delete unknown emails. But I opened this one. And I am glad that I did. It was from Debi, Arthur Jibillian's daughter, who never responded to my message a year earlier. It said:

"It's been almost a year since you sent me a note in Facebook and yet I just go it today-or at least saw it. My apologies-not sure where it was, but if I can help you in any way, if it's not too late, please let me know . . ."

Coincidence that I got her email, a year later, the very same day that I was going to give up on my book? I think it was something else . . . So I continued working and finished my book. A special thank you to Debi for responding to my request, it gave me the motivation to move forward and finish.

I'd also like to thank Scott Springer for designing the book cover-what would I have done without you! I'd also like to thank Father Dragomir Tuba for allowing me access to the endless amount of information in the Church library.

My hope is that this book educates as many people as possible about the Halyard Mission. Although this is a historical fiction piece, it is based on the true stories of actual US Airmen and tells their story through the eyes of one soldier. I hope you enjoy it!

"The ultimate tragedy of Draza Mihailovic cannot erase the memory of his heroic and often lonely struggle against the twin tyrannies that afflicted his people, Nazism and Communism. He knew that totalitarianism, whatever name it might take, is the death of freedom. He thus became a symbol of resistance to all those across the world who have had to fight a similar heroic and lonely struggle against totalitarianism. Mihailovic belonged to Yugoslavia; his spirit now belongs to all those who are willing to fight for freedom.

". . . the abandonment of allies can never buy security or freedom. In the mountains of Yugoslavia, in the jungles of Vietnam, wherever men and women have fought totalitarian brutality, it has been demonstrated beyond doubt, that both freedom and honor suffer when firm commitments become sacrificed to false hopes of appeasing aggressors by abandoning friends."

—President Ronald Reagan, September 8, 1979

CHAPTER 1

Summer 1943

"Let's go through this one more time, boys," said General MacKenzie as he walked across the front of the briefing room. The walls sported maps of Europe, Africa, and Asia, with Nazi occupied territories highlighted in urgent shades of yellow. Allied airmen, a mix of American and British soldiers, filled the room, anxiously awaiting the instructions for their next mission.

"The Ploesti Oil fields in Romania, located thirty miles north of Bucharest, are a major oil supply to Hitler and the Axis. They provide nearly a third of the oil that fuels their artillery. If we can put the fields out of commission, those Nazis will be hard pressed for the oil they need for fuel." He paused for a moment as he scanned the room. He focused on his men trying to remember every feature of every face present.

Although he was a patient man, who was well respected by all the airmen, he had a deep hatred of the Germans and anyone who allied with them. Rumor had it that during the First World War, the Germans shot and killed his best friend while he was unarmed and hooking up with a sweet little French girl. They killed the girl, too. General MacKenzie was never the same again.

"No disrespect intended, sir, but we've had missions like this a dozen times before. We fly in, drop our bombs, destroy our targets then turn right around and come back. Seems pretty simple to me! Like a slice of good old American pie" whooped Lieutenant Petrovich, who, at six feet four inches and just shy of 250 pounds, was one huge flying maniac. He loved his mama, his country, and flying more than anything in the world. And not necessarily in that order.

"You're right, we've had several missions similar to this. However, the Germans have tightened their protection around Ploesti. The last few missions, though relatively successful, came at a great cost to us." At the front of the briefing room, General MacKenzie paused, his white eyebrows burrowing over his pale blue eyes. "Those Nazis, as much as I hate to say it, are damn good shots. Too many of our men are getting shot down. Some to meet their Maker, God rest their souls, others to fall into the hands of the Germans, their Romanian friends or the Yugoslavs. And if they are getting in the hands of the Nazis or Chetniks, then they would have been better off meeting their Maker." The impending silence in the room intensified his next words.

"These missions are of grave importance. Our success," the General paused, "or failure, will greatly impact our ability to win this war once and for all. As such, we are increasing the intensity of our attacks. This is risky, boys. Much more so than I think you all understand."

So risky that FDR himself had to approve it. Hitler surrounded the refineries for miles with an enormous supply of anti-aircraft guns and fighters. The Axis would go to any length to protect the oil fields. The President struggled with approving the mission because of this. Who could guess how ruthless they would be on Allied planes attempting to destroy them? In the end, the overall benefit of killing their oil supply outweighed the potential risks. Regardless, thought the General, these boys had a right to know what they were getting in to.

"The previous bombings caused enough damage to say they were successful. However, to really be effective and to cripple the refineries, we are changing our strategy. We are going in for an all out attack." Some of the airmen whooped shouts of approval at the General's words. "As a joint Allied mission, we plan on hitting them and hitting them HARD." To emphasize his point, the General slammed his fist on the desk. "As you all know, our previous missions were conducted at levels thousands of feet in the air. Well, this time, you will be going in at very low levels. Low enough to graze a tree if you're not careful."

The room went silent. Although the airmen were well trained, maybe even some of the best trained in the world, they knew that with each mission there was a chance it could be their last. Flying at levels that low substantially increased the risk of not returning to base.

The General looked across the room and saw Petrovich look up and study the map of Eastern Europe, obviously contemplating the risks. The flight over Yugoslavia to Romania looked quick enough, but the low level flights added an additional element of danger that none of them could deny.

"Excuse me General. If we fly that low won't the oil fires from the exploding refineries threaten us too? And at that altitude, won't the Germans have an even easier target to shoot?" Robert Torreti, a young airman from New York, stood up and asked.

The General acknowledged the truth of Torreti's words with a nod, "But I have enough confidence in each of you airmen and the training that you have received to know that this is a mission you can accomplish." Torretti nodded and sat down. Some airmen murmured their agreement, while others silently questioned the sanity of the mission.

General MacKenzie slowly surveyed the room. As he made

eye contact with each of his men, he walked around to the front of his desk, shook his head and sighed. "However, I won't lie to you. This mission is dangerous. There's no doubt about it. But it is what you have all been trained - well trained - to do.

"As for the specifics, we will have approximately one hundred and seventy-seven B-24's completing this mission, known as Operation Tidal Wave. In an effort to minimize risk and maximize damage to the refineries, we will be having more than the usual mission preparations. As such, you will all be practicing low-level flights on a full-scale replica that we have built in the Libyan Desert. You will practice the flights and navigation until *perfection*. And this will all be done under strict radio silence. STRICT." The radio silence, they knew, was to decrease their chances of getting shot down.

"Sir. When do we go out?" Captain Bill O'Donnell asked. The General knew this wouldn't be the Captain's first time on a dangerous mission. Born to fly, O'Donnell was both skilled and brave, but never stupid. He kept his crew's safety in mind during each flight. And just like his friend Petrovich, winning one for his country and putting those Nazis out of business was something he couldn't wait to do.

O'Donnell was eager to get this mission started as it was just one step closer to ending this war and going home. He never realized how much he loved his lumpy old mattress until he had to sleep on the military issued cots. Once this war was over, O'Donnell would be eating his mother's apple pie and snuggling up to a one of a kind American girl. Just that thought alone kept his focus on successfully accomplishing this crazy mission. Knowing Petrovich was just as eager to get back home to his girl, O'Donnell glanced at him, gave a friendly grin and winked. Petrovich shook his head and smiled.

"O'Donnell, son, we have a lot of practice ahead of us to get this right. We don't have a lot of time, but we need to make sure that we wipe out as many refineries as possible, while getting you safely back to base. The timing of the mission will be based on when we feel that you have all perfected our strategy." Anticipating O'Donnell's protest, the General looked directly at him and shook his head. He needed O'Donnell, and the rest of his men, to fully understand what this mission meant to the Allied cause, and he needed them to prepare better than they had ever prepared before. There was no room for error.

"I appreciate your eagerness to go out. But I want you all to remember a few key points, in the event you don't make it back to base." The General felt a burst of fatherly pride as he looked out at the group of men. Each mission could be their last, yet they took on each one with brave determination.

He took a sip of his coal black coffee, closed his eyes and grinned. "I think the Italians have us beat on coffee, that's for sure." He opened his eyes and looked up at the map of Eastern Europe. He pointed to Romania and then slid his finger down, southwest, over Yugoslavia. "As I was saying earlier, getting shot down over Yugoslavia is a tricky thing boys. Depending on whom you run into, it could be heaven or hell.

"If by the grace of God, you find yourself with Tito's Partisans, count your lucky stars. For as much as I hate the Communists, I hate the Nazis more. And the Chetniks are in collaboration with them and their Italian friends."

The General wasn't too happy about this. Not too long ago, the Allies were supporting the Chetniks and their leader, General Mihailovic with weapons and men. In fact, Mihailovic was their key ally in the region. But recent intelligence, that the General privately questioned, indicated that he had been dealing and negotiating with the enemy while Tito and his communist Partisans had been pushing hard and attacking the Germans.

Word was that the Chetniks, with their bushy beards and large burly builds, were ruthless and brutal. Story after story came in describing acts of torture and cold-hearted killings. Although these stories were the complete opposites of earlier descriptions of Mihailovich and his men, the General knew that all too often, war had the unfortunate ability to bring out the savage side of man. And he had no choice but to trust the intelligence that confirmed these stories.

General MacKenzie walked around the desk and sat on the edge and continued. "Our focus needs to be on the preciseness and accuracy of this mission. Not to mention the radio silence. That'll help get us in. But don't be fooled, the Germans know we want those fields removed . . . permanently. They will be guarding them - they ARE guarding them - with the tenacity of a mother bear guarding her cubs."

The General stood up and added, "And if you get shot down in Yugoslavia, look for the Partisans. They will make sure you are safe. If you are in the hands of the Germans or Chetniks, remember your training and know we will do our best to get you out." He paused for a moment then added, "And it wouldn't hurt to pray for mercy. Dismissed."

*   *   *

"What do you think?" asked Petrovich. The mess hall had already emptied out from the morning's breakfast. A handful of airmen sat throughout the hall discussing the morning's briefing.

"I think there's a good chance that a lot of our boys might not make it back." O'Donnell replied as he drank his Coca Cola. He crunched on the ice and thought about the many friends he had already lost in this war.

"Hell, who knows, maybe we'll all be lucky and come back without a scratch." Petrovich crossed his fingers.

"Yea, maybe." But O'Donnell knew that was unlikely.

"You know, Petrovich, I'm not too sure about this one. It

seems like the stakes are too high. The Germans are ruthless as it is. Can you imagine what kind of fire power they will have when we come in like bats out of hell to attack their pot of gold?" "Can't say that I can. They fight hard for lesser things. I don't want to think about the fight they are going to give us. Without those fields, they can't win this war." Petrovich leaned forward, over the table, and shook his head. "This might be the one."

"The one?" O'Donnell asked as he also leaned forward, just inches from Petrovich.

"The one that takes us down" he replied.

Looking his friend in the eye, O'Donnell hoped he was wrong.

* * *

Several other airmen sat around the barracks, as well, contemplating the briefing and the information that the General had shared. They were both ripe and weary for the mission.

"I heard the Chetniks cut off a man's ears while he was alive then chopped his fingers off one at a time," said a soldier sitting under an open window.

"They burn down their own villages and turn over their women and children to the Nazis to torture," added another soldier.

While the soldiers related their stories, Red, the British flyer who'd joined them in Italy about six months ago, slowly stood up and looked around the room. His military haircut, as short as it was, could not diminish the bright red tint of his hair. As a result, his name quickly changed from Simon to Red. He was enjoying the stories about the Chetniks, if his smug smile was any indication.

"It's a shame that we spent so much time providing valuable artillery and manpower to Mihailovic. If we had not been so blinded by him, perhaps this godforsaken war would be over.

Or at least that much closer to the end." Many of the soldiers nodded in agreement.

"His Chetniks are ruthless monsters, as all of your stories have confirmed. His cowardly collaboration with the Nazi's was a slap in the face, after we have supported them for so long. Who knows what else he is capable of? I shudder at the thought. Allying ourselves with him was an enormous mistake." Red walked around the room, making eye contact with every man as he shared other stories of betrayal by the Chetniks.

"Tito is our man and when the time comes we must help him rid Yugoslavia of the Germans. Unfortunately, that is a topic for another day and another mission. As for today, at this moment, we must focus on the oil fields of Ploesti, and disrupting, or better yet, eliminating that oil supply to Hitler."

CHAPTER 2

August 1, 1943

THE EARLY MORNING light of the predawn hours of North Africa seeped through the windows of the briefing room. The men were gathered again, this time after two weeks of intensive practice flights. Confident that they were ready to fulfill their mission, they waited anxiously for the General's briefing to begin.

O'Donnell, Petrovich and Red, full from the hearty breakfast they ate before each mission, leaned against the back wall of the room. The air was heavy with nervous anticipation for the day's mission. Petrovich watched as the General strode to the front of the room. A map of Eastern Europe hung on the wall behind him.

"Good morning, men," he began. "Well, the intensive training you've completed is about to be put to the test. You will be flying out today to destroy as much of Ploesti as possible." He faced the map and pointed to Ploesti, Romania. The men listened carefully as he continued.

"Five groups will be traveling in formation from our current destination in North Africa to a town about sixty-five miles from Ploesti called Pitesti. The last of the five groups, which will be the 389th Bombardment Group, will turn slightly left to attack it's target at Campina," he moved his finger towards the left and stopped.

"The remaining four groups will fly to Floresti where they will then turn," he gestured towards the right, "and head for Ploesti. All four groups will simultaneously hit the oil fields at Ploesti and Brazi, then turn right and come home."

The General outlined a few additional specifics of the mission as the men listened at full attention. The dangers of the day's mission were very clear, even though they sounded simple. So many things could go wrong at any given time.

"That's it, boys. You're ready for this. Dismissed."

The airmen slowly exited the briefing room and headed out towards their planes to board and await their signal to take off. Red left the room first, followed by Petrovich and O'Donnell. Petrovich slowed his pace to allow the others to pass him. O'Donnell glanced back at him and slowed to allow Petrovich to catch up to him.

"What's wrong?" asked O'Donnell.

"The mission sounds easy enough. Right?"

"Sure, man. We know this one's got more danger written all over it. But we've run through it so many times, we could all probably fly to Romania with our eyes closed and still be fine," answered O'Donnell.

"I know. Just something about it, that's all. I think I've had enough of the flights. We're pretty close to our flight limit. I'm about ready for it."

"I'm right there with you. But until then, we need to stay focused on what we're here for. Don't overthink it. Just go out there, be alert and come home." O'Donnell said as he shifted to the right and headed towards his plane.

"You too," replied Petrovich. Feeling better for saying it out loud to his friend, he zipped his flight suit and jogged towards his plane.

His ten crewmembers were already on the B-17 bomber, in their positions, waiting for the signal. They were dressed in their thirty-pound flak suits and steel helmets that were designed to protect against enemy fire. Since parachutes were too bulky to wear all the time, they were also sporting the harness that allowed them to quickly clip on their parachutes when needed.

Petrovich sat in the cockpit next to his co-pilot and checked his instruments to ensure everything looked good. He was a good pilot and felt confident in the cockpit. As he ran through his routine check, his nerves calmed and he focused on the mission.

"We need to be extra alert this morning. The Germans will be pissed as hell when they see us. I expect them to come at us from all sides," Petrovich announced to his crew. "Let's pray that the long range fighters escorting us there and back can hold them off long enough for us to do our drop and get the hell out of there."

The planes and crews were ready to go. The engines roared to life and they waited for their turn to take off. Since the planes were unheated and temperatures could dip at their cruising elevation to as low as sixty degrees below zero, the men wore electronically heated suits that plugged into the plane. In preparation for the inevitable cold, they donned their heavy gloves, glad to have the warmth they would provide.

His turn to move, Petrovich sped down the runway, relishing in the intense speed of his aircraft. As the plane soared into the sky, he continued checking his gauges and instruments, looking for any sign of trouble.

At ten thousand feet, to compensate for the drop in oxygen levels, Petrovich and his men put on their oxygen masks. They continued climbing to their desired elevation. Once they reached it, Petrovich spoke to Ellison, his bombardier.

"Ellison, you comfortable down there?" joked Petrovich.

The bombardier sat right in the Plexiglas nose of the plane. He could see everything laid out below him.

"As ever. Got my eyes open, sir. I won't let one near us. Had an extra cup of coffee this morning. Just to be sure . . ." he joked back.

"Glad to hear it. Let's be safe. Once over the Mediterranean, we pass Yugoslavia and we're there. As we approach the mountains that separate Albania from Yugoslavia, we will start lowering our elevation. We've got some time, but stay alert anyway."

"Just enjoying the view for now, sir."

As they approached enemy territory, the jokes stopped, replaced by the roaring hum of the engine. Anxious anticipation was thick in the air as ten sets of eyes searched the skies for enemy defenders, armed with machine guns, canons and rockets. They looked for any and all signs of the enemy. Even on the ground, because the heavy antiaircraft fire from the ground was just as much as threat as the enemy fighters.

Once they reached the Yugoslav-Albanian border, the sky was thick with heavy clouds, which prevented them from flying at the preferred lower route through the mountains. Petrovich adjusted his route and elevation accordingly.

"The first two groups are pulling away too quickly." Petrovich whispered, "Something's not right." He was trained to maintain his position at all costs, so that is what he did. But the gap between the first two groups and these last three groups was getting too big.

He returned his attention to his mission. They were headed for Floresti first and then to Ploesti. He verified his coordinates and confirmed that they were nearing Floresti. He turned the plane slightly to the right and headed towards Ploesti.

"Flak below!" shouted Ellison. He watched as the flak exploded beneath the plane. The different colored puffs looked almost pretty as they made a soft colored cushiony pattern below. But they knew better. It was dangerous.

Something on the ground caught Petrovich's eye. "I'll be a son of a gun. That train is shooting at us!" Johnson turned and looked on the ground and saw a specially designed flak train. The freight cars dropped their sides and revealed anti-aircraft artillery. The train raced in tandem with their planes and spewed bullets from its guns at them.

"We're almost there!" shouted Petrovich. As he maneuvered the plane towards the oil fields, screaming in from his right a 20 mm cannon shell exploded just in front of the nose of his plane. The Plexiglas shattered and his intercom broke from the impact of the explosion. The plane jerked hard to the left from the waves of the explosion. He steadied the plane and continued forward.

"German fighters are swarming in!" Ellison shouted. But Petrovich saw them first. Hundreds of German fighters were flying towards them. The Allied fighters surrounded and defended Petrovich and the others, freeing them to focus on their targets.

The bombers ahead of him in the formation had already reached their destination. Without his intercom, Petrovich had to shout instructions to his crew.

"Target is in view. Just a few minutes now!"

Kaboom! The oil fields began exploding in front of his eyes. Petrovich watched as those bombers that had already reached the oil fields explode along with the oil fields.

"What's going on?" The oil fields exploded before the planes had a chance to drop their bombs. Something wasn't adding up. Petrovich watched in horror as plane after plane went up in flames as the oil refineries combusted one by one.

"Delayed-action bombs! Did our other guys get here first?" Petrovich reasoned. He didn't have time to think. "Bombs away!" they dropped the bombs on their targets and got the heck out of there.

CHAPTER 3

Spring 1944

OPERATION TIDAL WAVE was a DISASTER-one of the deadliest Allied missions of the war. Looking back now, Petrovich could name a dozen reasons why the mission failed. Lack of proper planning, poor execution, under estimating the enemy, and plain bad luck were just a few.

On one hand, they were able to get in and do some serious damage. They destroyed over 42% of the refinery capacity. On the other, the cost was much worse than they had ever anticipated. The sheer number of losses (fifty-four aircraft and five hundred and thirty-two airmen killed or missing) made him shudder. But the fact that he was able to sit here now and reflect upon it, to think of those men and their families, made him thankful.

He could have been one of them. Heck, he almost was one of them. But he was able to pull out of the attack just in time to make it back to base. His Liberator was severely damaged and he knew it was only by the grace of God that he and his crew made it back. The German antiaircraft fire came at him from what seemed all sides. He weaved through the bullets and smoke, blinded half the time. After what felt like a lifetime or two, he finally got the plane out of the line of fire.

He wasn't arrogant enough to say it was his mastered flying skills alone. Regardless, he was here, so were O'Donnell and Red. But poor Torretti didn't make it back. A German fighter came at him with no mercy. Bullets barraged though his bomber, killing his gunner instantaneously. Petrovich saw, through the smoke and haze, Torreti's plane spiral out of control and explode as it hit the ground.

The others were at the wrong place at the wrong time. The clouds over Yugoslavia wreaked more havoc than he originally thought. The first two groups of bombers had a sixty mile gap from the others. That was the beginning of a series of mistakes. The first groups mistook the town of Targoviste for Floresti and turned too soon. They reached Bucharest before they realized their mistake. Unfortunately, that was the headquarters for the Romanian air defenses. They alerted Ploesti before the bombers could reach their target.

They continued on to Ploesti and dropped delayed action bombs onto the refineries. Unfortunately, they didn't realize that Petrovich's groups were right behind them. Those delayed action bombs exploded as the bombers flew above and killed hundreds of Allied airmen. It was complete and utter chaos. A horror that he didn't think he would ever forget.

Restless from waiting, he rose and walked across base. He looked around and contemplated the bustle of activity. Everyone had a purpose. And they knew what they were there to do. Focus. That's what it was: focus. And determination. Determination not only to win the war, but to also live through it. For most, it started as the desire to stand up and do the right thing and stop the bloodshed. At least for Petrovich it started out like that.

Before he enlisted, he was deeply interested in the war. He read about it every day in the newspaper and talked about it with his father over dinner. He sat at the local diner with his friends and heatedly discussed Hitler's maniacal desire to take over Europe. Plus, he'd felt an immense sense of pride when he heard that the Yugoslavs were fighting Nazi occupation tooth and nail. Both of his parents were Serbian immigrants who fully embraced America and were committed to raising their children as Americans. But they also wanted their children to fully understand their heritage and to be proud of it as well.

That sense of pride grew even more when General Mihailovic was named one of TIME Magazine's men of the year for bravely leading the Serbs of Yugoslavia in a campaign of guerilla warfare resisting Nazi occupation. Though he wouldn't admit it now, that was one of the reasons he enlisted. Every time he looked at that cover page, he thought of his ancestors and how they always rose to the challenge and fought for what was right.

Then Pearl Harbor was attacked. That swell of pride for being of Serbian descent was quickly replaced by national pride of being an American. He was furious that his country, America, had been attacked. Sucker punched by the Japanese. He read and re-read the newspaper articles outlining the damage and destruction. He enlisted the next week. His mama cried, his dad slapped him on the back and then hugged him in that way that men do, and told him that he was proud of him. His sister, who already worshiped his every move, told everyone that her brother was going to show those Germans, Japanese and Italians who was boss! Heck, in her eyes, he was a war hero before the ink on the enlistment paperwork dried. He was determined to not only fight for his country, but to win this war for America and all it represented too.

Smiling at the memory, Petrovich put his hands in his pockets and contemplated the decision he made to join the fight against the Axis.

He knew he wanted to join the Air Force. Who wouldn't want to fly a plane and look so good doing it! And lucky for him, his aptitude for the skills necessary for flying naturally put him in that role. Training wasn't easy - there were days he thought he'd made the worst decision of his life. But overall, even through the worst days of training, he knew this is what he was born to do. Every time he went up, it was as if he was going back to where he belonged. He loved it. He couldn't imagine doing anything else in this war.

Although he loved what he did, he was tired of the war. Tired of seeing friends die. Tired of hearing the horror stories of torture and killing. What started out as a heartfelt mission to right the wrongs of the world was becoming something else.

Wanting to stop the Nazis hadn't changed. But each time he went out on a mission, he knew that the probabilities were working against him. Each flight was another that was either closer to his death or closer to going home. It was like a flip of a coin. And those chances didn't appeal to him very much at all.

Contemplating this, he opened his eyes and he saw O'Donnell and started walking towards him. He was leaning against the wall, his arms crossed over his chest, staring out into the sky. O'Donnell was his closest friend in this war. They didn't start out that way, but war had a way of creating bonds between unlikely people.

"What are you thinking about?" Petrovich asked as he leaned against the wall next to O'Donnell.

"My mother's cinnamon apple pie. She liked to put vanilla ice cream on top of it when it was warm. The ice cream would melt over the sides of the pie. " He licked his lips and smiled. "Man, I could go for a slice of that right now."

"Soon enough. But I seriously can't believe that you're thinking about apple pie." Petrovich laughed. "Me? I'm thinking about the girls back home. I can't wait to kiss a few!"

O'Donnell grinned. "Don't worry about me, my friend. I do

my share of thinking about those American pretties too. But right now, I'm thinking about my mother's apple pie."

"My mama loves to bake too. When she came to America she bought a cookbook of American recipes and tried a different one on my dad every day. He used to joke that he ate more American food than his American born friends." Petrovich smiled at the memory. "But nothing beat the days she decided we needed to have a taste of the 'old country.' After those hearty meals, she would pull out her homemade desserts. Now that I'm thinking about it, I think I'll eat ten pounds of those desserts when I get back home."

"I'll make you a deal" O'Donnell said and extended his hand to Petrovich. "When we get home, you come to my mother's house and try her cinnamon apple pie. And I'll go to your mama's house and try those old country desserts. My bet is that your mama will be asking for that apple pie recipe." Petrovich laughed and shook his hand.

"You're on. But it'll be your mother who will be learning a thing or two from my mama!" It was an old joke between them: something to think about other than the war going on around them. Friendly competition to make the days pass was better than thinking this might be the last time they saw each other or spoke.

They leaned against the wall in comfortable silence, taking in the activity around them. They would both be going out on another mission in the early morning hours.

Although the infamous Operation Tidal Wave was a failure, the Ploesti bombing raids continued. They learned their lessons and corrected what they could. Regardless, many of their fellow airmen were still shot down during those missions. But the missions continued, and will continue, until the last oil field was gone.

Shorter than Petrovich, O'Donnell, at 5'10" and 150 lbs.,

barely came up to Petrovich's shoulders. But what he lacked in height and weight, he made up in talent. He'd also gone out on that doomed Tidal Wave mission and made it back alive. O'Donnell also knew that the hands of God brought him and his crew back safely, but he kept that thought to himself. He didn't want anyone to think that he ever questioned his own flying ability.

It wasn't as if he thought he couldn't do it. In fact, the opposite was true. He *knew* he was good. Heck, so did everyone else. And in his humble opinion, why change that? He loved being recognized as one of the best. And he wanted to keep it that way.

Where Petrovich joined the fight for patriotic reasons, O'Donnell joined for others. He also heard about the war, read the papers and discussed the wrath of the Germans with his friends. But he always considered it a European problem, one that seemed to repeat itself every so many years. It wasn't as if he didn't care about the plight of the countries being plundered by Hitler. But he cared more about America, Americans and what they had to deal with at home. He felt the war was a world away, and he had more important things to worry about. Like if the Cubs were ever going to win the World Series.

However, he had been out with friends at the lake one evening. While they were there, he looked up and saw his best friend's sister running towards him. As her tear-streaked face came closer, his heart began to beat faster. Immediately, he knew something was wrong. She was usually laughing and silly. He never saw her cry.

"Billy! Billy!" she screamed. She ran right into him and threw her little arms around his waist, pushing her face into his stomach, sobbing. "Billy. It's Jack. They ca . . . ca . . . came . . ." her words faded into another sob. O'Donnell's heart had beat faster in his chest as pressure began to build deep within him. He gently pried her off and kneeled down to look her directly in the face. He took a moment to take a deep breath, scared that his fear would show when he spoke.

"What's up, Shorty? What's wrong with Jack? Who came?" he asked softly, but deep down he already knew the answer.

"Some men came to the door. I answered it and they asked for my mom." She paused to catch her breath. Her tears started flowing again as she continued, "They told my mom that Jack was a very brave soldier and that we should be proud of him. That he died honorably defending freedom. He DIED, Billy! Jack's dead!" she screamed. "I hate them! I hate them! Why did he have to go? Why?"

He just sat there and comforted her, as her brother would have done if he were there. He tried to remain calm for her sake. But deep inside, his sorrow was deep. It was as if his entire world had been swallowed by a black hole. There was no escape from the blackness around him.

Jack was the brother he never had. When the war started, Jack was obsessed with it. Where O'Donnell dismissed it as a European problem, Jack felt that America needed to step in and stop the madness. It was an argument they had often. When the opportunity arose for him to enlist, he did. O'Donnell thought he was crazy. Jack couldn't wait to go. Now he was dead.

That sorrow eventually turned into deep seeded anger. And that anger is what made him join the war. He wanted them to pay. He wanted them to suffer for what they did to Jack. So he enlisted with revenge on his heart. And it showed.

He came in with a chip on his shoulder and didn't care to make new friends. He was here on a mission: avenge his best friend. And that was Petrovich's first impression of him: cold, arrogant and distant. But as time went by, and the missions completed successfully, O'Donnell's personality began to warm. He changed his personal mission from that of revenge to that of doing what Jack would have wanted him to do. He was doing it for Jack and what Jack believed in. As he changed his perspective, so did his relationship with Petrovich. They became friends. Now there wasn't anyone either of them trusted more.

Red walked by with one of the British Special Operations Executives (SOE). The SOE was established by Winston Churchill to connect to resistance movements throughout Europe. The thought was to have them infiltrate and work with those movements to fight the Germans from within occupied territories. They worked closely with the American version, known as the OSS, Office of Strategic Services. When it came down to it, the OSS and SOE were spies. Their agents used espionage to fulfill their missions. Petrovich had his doubts about them. But he didn't express them to anyone other than O'Donnell who hadn't yet made up his mind about them.

Red and the agent were having a heated discussion, at least from the looks of it. The OSS agent looked up and saw Petrovich and O'Donnell. He abruptly stopped his conversation with Red and waved. Red turned and looked over his shoulder at them and nodded.

"Afternoon, Gentlemen. Taking some well deserved rest today before tomorrow's mission?" O'Donnell's smile didn't quite reflect in his eyes as he looked up.

"Just thinking, Red. Just thinking . . ." O'Donnell didn't really care too much for Red. He couldn't put his finger on it, but there was something about him that made him want to look over his shoulder whenever they were near each other. Red was a good pilot. He'd made it back from several missions too. And each mission was successful. But he made O'Donnell's skin crawl.

"Americans are so thoughtful." He said to the SOE agent as they continued walking away. They chuckled at the private joke, waiting to continue their original conversation until they were far enough away.

"What is it about him that makes me feel like I need to take another shower?" Petrovich questioned as he pretended to wipe something off of his arms and legs. "I didn't recognize the guy he was with."

"I think it's one of those British spies," O'Donnell shook his head at the thought.

"Who cares anyway? I've got more important things to think about. I have a bad feeling about tomorrow's mission." Petrovich put his hands in his pockets and rocked forward off of the wall. "Just can't shake this feeling."

"It'll all be good. It always is. We are two of the best pilots here. Remember that." O'Donnell stretched his arms over his head and grinned at Petrovich. "We go out again in the morning, take care of business, and come back. Then, tomorrow over dinner, I'll remind you that I am the better pilot."

Petrovich laughed at the old joke and shook O'Donnell's hand. "Brother, sounds good to me. But we both know who's the better pilot here, and it's not you!" As he stepped forward, Petrovich still couldn't shake his uneasy feeling. Walking away, he said a silent prayer and hoped that O'Donnell was right.

CHAPTER 4

*T*HICK BLACK SMOKE *filled the room. He lifted his hands and tried opening his eyes, but the smoke was too thick, he couldn't see his hand in front of his face. Where was the door? He thought he remembered it was to his left, so he lay down on the floor and started crawling that way. Taking a deep breath, he choked. The smoke burned his airways as he coughed it back out. He had to be smart, stay as low to the ground and take small shallow breaths.* Where is that door? *He had to get to it soon or he'd die. Sweat was dripping over his forehead and down his cheeks. He finally reached the wall. No door. Was it the other way? Panic overcame him so he stood, eyes still closed, blindly running in the other direction. No door. He started pounding on the wall with both fists. Wasn't there a window? How could there be no door?*

He kept pounding on the wall. He tried to scream for help, but no sounds came as the smoke filled his lungs. He gasped as the burning in his chest became too much to take. "I don't want to die like this," was his last thought as he collapsed to the ground, screaming silence.

Petrovich's body jerked forward out of bed, his hands clutching his throat as he gasped for air. His undershirt was drenched. His eyes darted around the room. Dawn had yet to break through, but the light from the full moon provided enough for him to see the door and the window on the other side of the room. As his eyes adjusted to the dim moonlight, he realized that it was only a dream. The tangled mess of blankets wrapped around his legs, trapping him in bed. He untangled himself and hurried outside. As soon as he was outside he took a deep breath of fresh air to try and calm his heart, which was pounding so hard he would have sworn it was going to beat right out of his chest. He closed his eyes and forced his breath to slow.

The dream was worse tonight than it had ever been. The other nights he'd been able to wake up before he realized there wasn't a door or window from which to escape. Tonight he caught a glimpse of his death. Not a great way to start the day, especially during wartime, right before a mission.

"I've got to get a grip. It's just a dream." Petrovich muttered to himself. Out of the corner of his eye, he saw something move. He took a better look, trying to let his eyes adjust, and didn't see anything. As he turned back towards the bunkhouse, he saw it again. "What the heck?" he whispered. It couldn't have been past 2 a.m. Who would be out at this hour?

He walked down the narrow corridor between the buildings. The lights were all off, but with the full moon he could still see clearly. Nothing. The dream spooked him enough to see things in the shadows. He turned around and walked back towards his bunkhouse when something shiny caught his eye. He bent down to pick up the red and gold star-shaped pendant. He wondered how he hadn't seen it earlier. It was vaguely familiar, but he couldn't place it. It seemed so out of place here. It wasn't a medal of honor any of the Allies used. In the morning, he'd ask around and see if anyone knew what it was or who it belonged to.

He returned to his bunk and lay down. He needed to try to

get in at least another couple of hours of sleep before heading out to start the day's Ploesti raid. Staring at the star, he turned it over and around in his fingers. As he slowly drifted back to sleep, the star slipped from his fingers to the floor. And he dreamt of red stars, black smoke and a skull and cross bones.

*   *   *

At dawn, O'Donnell was up and ready to go. He was surprised at how good he slept, just like a baby. That's a good omen, he thought. He hadn't slept that good in so long; it must mean that this bombing run will be another safe one. He kept reminding himself that he survived Op Tidal Wave. If he survived that, he could survive anything. He still knew that each time they went out, it was a risk. But he had a good crew and they worked well together.

Being the pilot meant more than just flying the plane. The job came with a lot of responsibility. The men were in his hands. His crew was important to him. They were tight knit each placing his life in the hands of the others. He not only wanted to make sure that he made it back to base in one piece, but that his men did too. That weighed on his conscience. The responsibility for their lives was what kept him focused. He didn't want to be the reason his men didn't make it back alive.

Dressed and ready to go, he walked towards the B-24 bomber. The sun was just starting to rise behind the huge plane. It wasn't designed to be hidden from the enemy, that's for sure. In fact, the opposite was true. Its enormous size made it an easy target for the Germans. But it had to be big to carry as many bombs and crew members as it did. Each flight carried the pilot and co-pilot, who would take over if the pilot was injured or killed. Then there were the bombardier, navigator, engineer, radioman, nose gunner, ball gunner, waist gunner and tail gunner. Each job was as important as the rest.

O'Donnell saw Petrovich and walked over to him. "Hey, ready to do this?" he asked.

"As always."

"I slept like a baby last night. I feel real good about this one. How about you? You don't look so good."

"I slept like crap. Woke up in the middle of the night, nearly screaming like a girl. Stupid dream again. This war's getting to me." Petrovich rubbed his hands over his face and shook his head.

"No worries, man. You and your crew are some of the best. " He paused and looked over at the planes. "This war is getting to all of us. Some more than others. It will end-eventually. And each time we go out, we get that much closer to going home. You can't go out there worried about this dream. You'll lose your focus."

"I know. I know. Too bad for those Germans that even on only a few hours of sleep, I'm still better than most of what they've got!"

"That's what I'm talking about! Come one, let's get this thing done. Then when we get back, I'll tell you all about my dream about this gorgeous little Italian girl I met." He winked "Now, that's the kind of dream you wish you had!" He smacked Petrovich on the back and headed towards his plane.

Everyone was in his place except for Johnson, the ball gunner. He had to wait until after take off to climb out of the fuselage into his tiny Plexiglas sphere beneath the bomber. As everyone got into place, O'Donnell focused on his instruments, climbing higher in altitude. To his right the co-pilot, Richardson, sat unusually quiet.

"Why so quiet this morning?"

"Just thinking about what Axis Sally said last night, did you listen to her?" he asked, not waiting for a reply. "In that sexy voice of hers, she was going on and on about how we are the aggressors and that we should be ashamed for what we are doing. I don't get it. How can she be so blind?"

Axis Sally was an American woman who had fallen in love with a German man and moved to Germany. She broadcasted German propaganda from a Berlin radio station. In between songs, she would send messages to the Allied men trying to demoralize them

"Who knows? Whatever her reasons are, she's a traitor. But even as a traitor, she plays some real good music."

"That she does. We all know what she says is crap. But we all listen anyway. It's got to be the music, well that and just hearing that sexy American voice. God, I miss hearing that."

The planes were in formation and flying towards Ploesti. At this altitude it got to be very cold in the plane. O'Donnell felt bad for Johnson. He really had the worst spot. It was so cramped in that sphere he could barely move. He had to wait until takeoff to get in and he had to get out before they landed. The ball gunners sometimes got frostbite on their ears from the extremely low temperatures. Johnson shifted in his electric suit. It was plugged into a 21-volt system to keep warm. But that didn't help the ears. Poor guy.

As they neared their target, the mood in the plane sobered. Everyone remembered that the Germans had heavy defenses around the refineries. At any given moment, there would be German fighter planes tearing through their formation. They just had to drop their bombs on target and head back.

O'Donnell looked out into the sky and thought how odd it was that it looked so peaceful when they were in the air, even as the sounds of the engines roared through the plane. It whispered peace, like the eye of the storm. It was a false feeling, he knew. But he enjoyed this short time they had in the air.

He was high on adrenaline. The closer they got to Ploesti, the faster his heart beat. This was it. This is when his skills would make it either life or death. Anytime now, the Germans would . . .

An antiaircraft bomb exploded in front of them, shaking the plane back and forth. Shells exploded all around them. Smoke and flak filled the air, as the plane jerked violently left and right. O'Donnell steadied the plane and continued heading towards the target, all the while trying to avoid the antiaircraft fire. The refineries were now in sight and grew as they quickly approached them.

"Bombs away!" yelled out the bombardier. Bulls-eye! Shockwaves rippled through the air as flames shot up from the explosion. The plane slammed hard to the left. Still trying to avoid German rockets, O'Donnell steadied their plane then tilted the wing down and turned the plane to head back to base.

A burst of bright orange and red flames exploded to their right. "Thompson's hit!" shouted Richardson. The plane shuddered violently from the force of the explosion and O'Donnell struggled to keep control. He would mourn those men later, but for now he had to get his crew out of this mess. Shells continued to explode all around them. He could barely see through the flak.

Once they made it past the danger zone, the crew began to relax. They'd made it through the worst part. O'Donnell knew they weren't safe yet. Shrapnel had done some damage to the plane, but not enough to take it down.

"We took some good hits this time." O'Donnell took at look at his controls then said, "We're losing altitude."

Still losing altitude, the plane fell out of formation. They could make it back like this, as long as they didn't get any surprise visits from the Germans. Without the protection of the formation they were like a sitting duck.

"We got lucky, you know. That was Thomson's plane and crew that went down. He's one of our best." Richardson didn't have to say it. O'Donnell was already thinking it. It could have been any of them. That was the risk they all took. They fell silent as they thought about the loss of lives and how thankful they were that it hadn't been them.

Suddenly, the plane shook violently. Antiaircraft fire exploded around them. O'Donnell struggled to regain control.

"What the . . . ? Where did that come from?" O'Donnell shouted as he caught a glimpse of enemy aircraft approaching them. Struggling to maintain control, the plane shook again.

"Fighters at six o'clock! And four o'clock!" shouted the tail gunner. They prepared for the attack, the gunners ready to defend. The Germans fired again; knocking the plane so hard it dropped ten feet.

"Johnson's been hit! He's been hit!" Johnson was slouched in his cramped space, shrapnel in his neck, his sphere filling with dark red blood. Panic erupted in the plane as the reality of attack began to sink in. O'Donnell and Richardson fought to avoid the continual explosions around them.

"We're dropping too fast. We're going to have to abandon ship." Richardson nodded in agreement. O'Donnell picked up the intercom and shouted out his command.

"Abandon ship! Abandon ship!" The command echoed over the intercom. Everyone quickly clipped their parachutes onto their harnesses and prepared to jump into the unknown. They knew they were somewhere over Serbia. But they didn't know what was waiting for them when they got there.

One by one they jumped out of the plane, Richardson and O'Donnell being the last two. Richardson paused before jumping.

"See you on the ground! Remember to look for the Partisans. They are our only hope at this point." Then he was out. O'Donnell said a short prayer and jumped.

CHAPTER 5

"ONE THOUSAND ONE, one thousand two, one thousand three." O'Donnell counted to himself as he plummeted towards the ground. At three, he thrust his hand and pulled the ripcord. Nothing. He pulled it again. Nothing. As realization emerged, he began to panic. He was falling even faster to the ground and his parachute wouldn't open. Trying to stay calm, he tugged as hard as he could on the canvas. He tried to take a deep breath, but his lungs weren't cooperating. Instead, he was breathing faster and faster. The breaths were coming so fast that he couldn't get any air into his lungs. Even though he was hyperventilating, he kept pulling on the canvas. With trembling hands, he violently tugged and tugged until it finally came loose. The parachute burst open above him, brutally yanking the harness, and stopping his heart-stopping free fall to the ground. As he floated through the sky and approached the ground, he succumbed to darkness.

"Pozurite! Nemamo puno vremena! Ajde!"
"Marko! Pazi tamo. Vidi da oni gadovi ne dolazu!"

The words were fuzzy and foreign. The voices drifted in and out as the tunnel of darkness that enveloped him slowly slipped away. Coming to, O'Donnell tried to open his eyes. He blinked several times as he tried to adjust to the blinding morning light. Attempting to focus, he could only make out several blurred figures around him. Where was he? Who were these people? Blinking several more times, his vision finally cleared. Two tall, bearded men, with khaki green, makeshift military uniforms, surrounded him.

"*Ej, probudio se!*" someone whispered excitedly.

"Who are you?" O'Donnell asked as they worked to free him of his parachute, which happened to be hanging in a low tree. He must have landed in the tree branches when he passed out. Looking down, he noticed two more similar looking men on the ground below.

"Do you speak English?" he asked again. The men glanced at him and kept on working to free him. Two of the men were up in the tree loosening him from his harness while two others were waiting below to catch him. *This can't be good*, he thought. *What are they going to do with me?*

"*Pazite!*" One of the men in the tree shouted.

With a jolt, O'Donnell fell to the ground. He landed on his feet but then he lost his footing and fell to his hands and knees. The men on the ground immediately put their hands under his arms and lifted him up to his feet, while the others struggled to pull the parachute out of the tree. One of the men standing with O'Donnell ran over to help them. After several frantic minutes of struggling to get it down, the parachute fell to the ground. They pulled it and hid it behind several nearby tall bushes.

Suddenly, they all stopped and stood very still. They put their fingers to their lips, a silent order to be quiet. They looked at O'Donnell and started whispering and pointing to the bushes. He couldn't understand what they were saying at first. But when they started dragging him over to the bushes, he understood. They wanted him to hide. An approaching car could be heard as it neared. He crouched to the ground and held his breath. He didn't know if these were the good guys or bad guys. All he could do at this point was try to figure out a way back to Allied men. And try hard not to get caught by the Nazis. Afraid breathing would give him away, he took a deep breath and waited.

The jeep stopped fifteen feet away from the bushes. Looking through the tangle of leaves, he saw that it was a German patrol. Two German soldiers spoke to each other for a few minutes while looking at the soldiers who had helped him. The Nazis got out of the jeep and quickly approached the men. O'Donnell still couldn't understand what they were saying, but he was sure that his rescuers were not Germans. The Nazis were speaking German and the others were speaking a Slavic language, more than likely Serbian. The Nazis were arguing with the men. They were pointing to the sky and gesturing with their arms. It was obvious that they were trying to say that something dropped from the sky and could have landed around here. The unknown men shrugged and shook their heads no.

After several minutes, the frustrated Germans returned to their jeep. Their faces contorted with anger as they shouted at the men. One of them took his finger and swiped it across his neck and pointed to the men before they drove off. When they were out of sight, the unknowns turned and gestured to O'Donnell to get up. He walked over to them, still leery, but it looked like they weren't planning on turning him over to the Nazis. At least not yet. That had to be a good sign.

"Who are you?" O'Donnell asked again. And once again blank stares as they were directing him to walk up the hill with them. It wasn't any use asking again. Instead, he just took in his surroundings to see if he could get any clues to his whereabouts. And he needed to figure out who his captors were. Were these guys Chetniks or Partisans? And where were they taking him?

They walked for hours, up and down steep hillsides, through forests and open fields, eventually stopping in a little hillside village. There were about a dozen little grey stone homes with red tiled roofs scattered throughout. In front of some of the homes were mule driven carts filled with hay or other items. The villagers were busy doing their daily chores, so at first they didn't notice them walking up. As they approached the first two homes, the villagers saw O'Donnell and his four captors and started towards them.

An elderly woman, wearing a dark wool vest over a white shirt and a black skirt hobbled up to him. Her sparkling green eyes looked at him warily beneath white eyebrows. Beneath the dark blue handkerchief tied around her heard, her long silver hair wisped across her wrinkled forehead. Placing hands on either side of his face she stared straight into his soul. Tears streamed down her cheeks.

"Dobro Dosao nas spasitelj! Amerikanac! Ti ces nas spasiti!" she cried and kissed his cheeks. *"Hvala Gospode Boze!"* He had no idea what the heck the woman said, except that he was confident that they knew he was an American. She wrapped her arms around him and squeezed tight. He surprised by the extreme show of affection.

The woman let go and walked towards an icon of a saint hanging on the outside entrance wall of one of the homes. She bent over and put the thumb, forefinger and middle fingers of her right hand together and placed them on her forehead, her belly, her right shoulder and then her left shoulder, making the sign of the cross. She did this three times and then kissed the icon.

"Does anyone here speak English?" he asked. No one answered him. The situation, though not as bad as it could've been, wasn't getting much better. He was hungry and his throat was raw from thirst. As if reading his mind, a little girl with her hair in a long braid down her back, walked towards him with a cup of cold water. She looked up at him with a shy grin and with both hands handed the tin cup to him.

"Thank you, sweetie," he said as he desperately drank the water. He leaned down and lightly tugged her braid. He gestured to the cup and then to his mouth, trying to find a way to ask for more water. The little girl smiled and grabbed the cup to refill it from a nearby well of water. When she returned, he drank the second cup as quickly as the first. She repeated the same motions he made earlier to ask for more. He shook his head as he bent down to say thank you. She jumped up and threw her arms around his neck and held on tightly with an unexpected show of affection.

"Hey, there, now. That's awfully sweet of you," he whispered as he untangled himself from her grasp. He wanted to ask her name, but knew she wouldn't understand. So instead, he pointed to himself and said, "Bill."

She looked at him curiously and then recognition lit up her eyes. She mimicked his gesture, pointing to her chest, and with a huge smile, she said, "Milka!"

"Well, Milka, thank you for the cold water!" Milka laughed and ran off towards a group of other children standing nearby. They huddled together, talking fast and pointing and staring at him. O'Donnell looked around and saw that the villagers had begun to disperse. The men who had brought him here were speaking to another older man. They glanced at him occasionally as they carried on their discussion. Finally, the older man gestured for him to come with them.

O'Donnell was feeling more comfortable with the situation. If they were Nazi collaborators, they would have turned him in earlier. And if they had any ill intentions, they surely wouldn't have brought him to the village and let the girl give him water. But he sorely wished he knew who these people were and if they could get him in touch with any other Americans or Allied men who might be nearby.

They entered what appeared to be the older man's home. Inside, they gestured for him to sit at a long wooden table. He pulled out one of the chairs, scraping the concrete floor, sat down and wondered when he was going to be able to eat. He figured he was safe for now and his stomach started to grumble. He didn't even realize how hungry he was until he sat down. Now that he knew it, he could eat enough for the whole Air Force. After several minutes, he was joined by the older man, his three young sons, and to his pleasant surprise, little Milka. Milka's mother was busy getting dinner together.

The men all sat at the table, while Milka and her mother served them. At first, O'Donnell didn't quite understand what was happening as they placed a small half loaf of bread, a card deck size piece of goat cheese, and lard on the table. The others patiently stared at him. He finally realized that they were waiting for him to eat. He took a piece of the bread and eagerly bit into it. To his dismay, it was stale and hard. But he took it gratefully and ate. He had never eaten goat cheese and found that he wasn't too crazy about it. But he was incredibly hungry and this was better than starving to death. He wasn't sure what they did with the lard, so he just left that alone.

He greedily devoured the small amount of food placed in front of him. As he chewed, he contemplated their choice of food and decided that they were more than likely giving him their scraps. He was a stranger to them, why share the good stuff? Who was he to judge anyway? As they say, beggars can't be choosers and at this point he'd take anything they could give him. After several minutes, he glanced at his hosts and realized that they hadn't started eating. It was only then that he realized that they were waiting for him to finish eating before they began. And they weren't going to be eating some delicious food they had on the side. They were going to share whatever he left for them. Ashamed, he pushed his plate back and thanked them for their kindness. Seeing he was finished, they took what was left, which wasn't much, and shared it amongst the five of them. He watched them as they quietly ate, savoring each morsel of food. The children listened eagerly as their father spoke, interrupting him only occasionally, and laughing every now and then. O'Donnell wasn't sure what the conversation was, but he enjoyed watching the way this family interacted. It reminded him of his home and his own family. They were worlds away from each other, but still so much the same.

Deep in thought, a sudden pounding on the door nearly startled O'Donnell off his chair. The father opened the door and a young, dark haired man stepped in. He said something to the family and they jumped up from their chairs. Milka and her mother scattered to hastily clean up dinner. The two men were in a heated discussion, their voices just this side of shouting. The young one pointed at O'Donnell as his voice boomed across the room. *What's that all about?* wondered O'Donnell.

The two men continued their discussion until the door swung open and the other man's child ran in. Struggling for a breath in between words, he tugged on the younger man's shirt. The men abruptly stopped their discussion and asked the boy a question. His head violently bobbed up and down. Milka's father dismissed the man and his son with another nod, and he closed the door immediately behind them.

He grabbed O'Donnell by the arm and dragged him to the other side of the room, stopping in front of a small bed. He pointed to the space beneath the bed and placed his forefinger over his mouth ordering him to be quiet. He was gesturing quickly now, pushing O'Donnell down. He crawled under the bed, barely fitting in the narrow space beneath. Just as he pulled his entire body underneath, there was a pounding on the door.

Milka's mother turned towards the icon of a saint on the east wall of the house, said a silent prayer and then crossed herself as O'Donnell watched the old lady do earlier. Milka grabbed her mother's dress and apron tightly. The boys sat quietly at the table, their faces pale with fear, as they watched their father cross himself before he slowly opened the door.

CHAPTER 6

P ETROVICH LOOKED OVER at his co-pilot, Graves, and gave him a thumbs up as they saw the Italian base slowly come into view. And boy was that a sight for sore eyes. He shifted the gears for their landing, waiting as each of the remaining planes in their formation landed.

"Prepare for landing" he called out to his crew as they began their descent to the landing strip. The buildings on base became larger as they quickly approached the ground. The landing gear engaged and he steadied the plane. Landing was such a rush. He never got tired of how he felt as the plane dropped towards the strip and the satisfaction he felt as he successfully landed back at base each time.

They slowed to a complete stop and disengaged themselves from the plane. Petrovich waited to be the last man to climb down the ladder out of the plane. It was a ritual meant to show his crew the respect they deserved for a job well done.

"Good job, boys" he exclaimed as they walked from the strip. They removed their helmets and Petrovich ran his fingers over his thick dark crew cut. "Not an easy task in that hell up there, but you all did good. Uncle Sam would be proud!" They laughed at the old joke. Petrovich said the same thing after every successful mission.

And was he happy to be on base this time! That was a close call. Those German fighters came out of nowhere, just as he thought they got through the worst of their defenses. He sadly remembered Thomson and his crew. He grieved for his fellow airmen, and prayed that their families could somehow find comfort and get past their inevitable grief.

"Tough break for Thomson and his guys" said Graves.

"Yea. He was a good guy. His wife had their baby right before he was deployed. He never even got to see his boy." Petrovich's voice was hoarse with sympathy.

"Man. That sucks. Those other guys were all right too. I hate that they had to go out like that. It's going to play over and over in my mind, the way that plane burst into flames." Graves shook his head as he unzipped his flying suit.

"It's been a long time since we've seen anything like that. But it never gets easier. I don't know if I will ever forget the sight of it." Petrovich switched the helmet from his right hand to his left and unzipped his suit.

"We're going to clean up and get out of these suits. Maybe meet up after the debriefing. You coming?" Graves asked.

"Maybe later. I'm going to get cleaned up myself. See you."

After he showered and changed, he headed out of the barracks. He decided to look for O'Donnell. They'd share their stories of the mission, like they always did. It had become a tradition, and a way to get past the stress and sadness when they lost some of their own. He walked across base and saw Red and one of the British SOE agents sitting at a table. They kept their voices low.

"Hey, you guys see O'Donnell?" he asked. They abruptly stopped their conversation as he came closer. Red glared at the initial interruption. But that was quickly replaced by a frown as he looked up at Petrovich. He looked back at the SOE agent and shook his head.

"Didn't you hear? They didn't make it back." Red replied staring at his hands on the table.

"What?" Petrovich froze. He didn't expect that. He slowly ran his hands over his head as he digested Red's response. His throat was suddenly too dry. "No, I just got back. I mean, I knew he was having some difficulty and had to fly low and out of formation, but I thought they made it back." Petrovich couldn't believe what he was hearing.

Willing himself to move, he placed his hands on the table and closed his eyes. Replaying the events of the day in his head, he couldn't remember when he last saw O'Donnell's plane. He looked at Red with apprehension. Fearing the worst for his best friend.

"When he fell out of formation, German fighters attacked. And from what we gathered, the plane crashed in Yugoslavia. There hasn't been any communication from them. I'm sorry, my friend. But it doesn't look good." Red put his hand on Petrovich's shoulder. "He's a good pilot. I know you two were close. I'm really sorry."

Petrovich stood there, not moving and barely breathing. He didn't want to believe that O'Donnell was dead. He stared at Red and the other Brit for a few long minutes, processing the information.

"Are you sure?" was all he could say. Red nodded slowly, confirming Petrovich's fears.

"All I know is that his plane went down. We don't know if they made it out as of yet." He paused for a few moments and scanned Petrovich's face. "If they did, and they found Tito's men, then they are OK and the Partisans will contact us. It's too early to know at this point." He looked at the SOE agent, a silent message passing between them.

Petrovich still couldn't believe it. He knew, each time they went out, that it could happen. But that didn't make it any easier to take. O'Donnell was his friend, and one of the best fliers they had. He hoped with everything he had, that he did parachute out and was in the right hands. Whoever that happened to be.

* * *

Red watched Petrovich as he walked away. He swallowed. Everyone knew the bond that he had with O'Donnell.

"Bloody shame to hear that a talented and brave flier went down like that," he said to the SOE agent.

"Bloody shame, for sure. But he was a bit volatile from what I've gathered." The SOE agent stretched his arms over his head.

"I'd heard he was a spit fire from the moment he entered this God-forsaken war. Hell bent on avenging his friend who'd been killed by the Germans. But he calmed with time. I think our boy Petrovich over there had some to do with that." Red replied as he rose to leave.

"Could be. Or maybe he mellowed with time." The SOE agent looked up at Red and continued. "Either way, he'd been a great flier, I hope he's alive and well with the Partisans. Otherwise, I don't think it'd be likely that any of us would see him again."

As Red walked away, he thought of the agent's words. Tito and his Partisans were the saving grace, and O'Donnell may be just lucky enough to meet Tito himself. That would be an honor to anyone. But these yanks don't fully see that yet, he thought. But they will. When the time is right, they will see.

* * *

Petrovich sat on his bunk. Elbows on knees, he covered his face with his hands. *God, I know that I haven't always been the one to pray and all that. And I'm sorry for that. But O'Donnell's a good guy - fighting for the good guys, trying to stop all the killing and bloodshed, that I'm pretty sure you don't like either. I'm asking, no I'm begging, that he's in good hands and safe.*

I don't have many friends like him. And I'd like to be able to see him again. So . . . I'm not even sure how to ask this. But, if you could do, what you do, and let him be safe. I'd very much appreciate it. I promise to go to Church more often when I'm home. I'm begging you to help my friend. Amen.

Petrovich opened his eyes and saw something shiny just below the bunk. He bent over and picked up the red and gold star pendant. He contemplated it for a few minutes. He was too tired last night to remember where he had seen it before. But now he remembered seeing stars like this on pictures of Soviet generals. What in the world would a Communist red star be doing on their base?

* * *

"General MacKenzie, sir." Petrovich saluted when he saw the General later in the day. "Have you received any contact from O'Donnell and his crew?"

"Not yet, son. But don't give up hope. It's early yet. We hope to get contact with them soon." General MacKenzie looked at him with thoughtful eyes. He knew what it was like to lose a good friend to the hatefulness of war.

"O'Donnell's a brave man. He's one of the top men we have. I have full faith that if he was able to get out of that plane, that he'd get to where he needs to be on the ground to be safe. But right now, we don't know if he made it out of the plane before it crashed. We just know that they were attempting to abandon ship. Now it's just a waiting game."

"Thank you, sir. Please keep me posted and let me know if, I mean when, he contacts us." Petrovich saluted the General and walked away.

CHAPTER 7

O'DONNELL HELD HIS breath as the door creaked opened. A German soldier forced his way into the home. Pushing Milka's father to the side, he walked towards the boys at the table. They jumped up out of their seats and quickly gathered around their father. The German's gaze shifted around the room, eventually stopping on the father. Trying to intimidate, the German stared at him for several seconds. After a long, uncomfortable stretch of silence, he finally asked him a question. His thick German accent sounded unnatural as he struggled to speak the Slavic language.

"Ne. Nema niko ovde, samo ja i porodica moja."

Milka's father shook his head as he answered the soldier. O'Donnell didn't know what he said, but he figured the German was asking about him, especially because he was sure he heard him say "Amerikanac." And he assumed that her father denied O'Donnell's presence in their home. He couldn't understand the continuing conversation, but he could see that they were still standing near the table. O'Donnell focused hard on keeping his body still, afraid that any movement would alert the soldier to his whereabouts. He was concerned for his life, but he was more worried for Milka and her family. O'Donnell shuddered to think what would happen to them if the soldier found out that they were hiding an American soldier.

Abruptly, the conversation ended and the German's shiny black boots meandered across the room. They paused by Milka and her mother. O'Donnell watched Milka move even closer to her mother and clutch her apron. He was ready to jump out from under the bed if the soldier laid a hand on that sweet little girl or her mother. As O'Donnell mentally prepared to attack, the black boots turned and sauntered towards the bed. They stopped right in front of O'Donnell's face.

This is it, he thought. *He's got me for sure.* O'Donnell held his breath and stared at the boots for an eternity. Suddenly, the German's boots turned around and walked briskly towards the door. He barked a few words and walked out.

Milka's father quickly locked the door behind the soldier and turned around to face the bed. He knelt down, coming into O'Donnell's view. He signaled to O'Donnell to wait another minute before coming out from under the bed. O'Donnell acknowledged the universal one finger symbol with a quick nod and waited, watching him to see what came next.

Her father ran to the other side of the room and peered out the window. Milka let go of her mom and ran to her father. He hugged her, comforting her in a quietly confident and soothing voice. She squeezed for a few minutes then finally let go. When he spoke to her again, she ran to the bed and knelt in front of O'Donnell. A wide grin spread across her pretty face as she waved him out from under the bed.

"That was a close call." O'Donnell sighed, saying it to no one in particular because he knew that they couldn't understand him anyway. "Thank you, er . . ." O'Donnell stumbled as he tried to find a way to communicate his appreciation.

"You are velcome" Milka's older brother grinned. O'Donnell's eyes bulged from his head. The boy laughed out loud.

"You speak English?"

"Yes, but very little. I learn little. No too good." The boy straightened his shoulders ever so slightly as he spoke, obviously proud of the little bit of English he knew.

"Well, thank you again. Tell your family that I am very grateful to them for not turning me in to that Nazi." The boy's eyebrows scrunched together as he struggled to understand what O'Donnell said, or maybe he was struggling to find the words to respond. Either way, O'Donnell was grateful to not be in the hands of the Nazis.

Milka's father said something and then pointed towards the bed. O'Donnell understood that meant he was being told to go to sleep and he welcomed it. The fatigue set in so fast that O'Donnell could barely keep his eyes open. He lay down on the bed and pulled the thick wool blanket up to his chin. Rolling onto his side, he watched as the children climbed into bed. Milka's mother kissed each of her children on their foreheads and tucked them in.

Seeing they were safely in bed, she laid some more wool blankets onto the cold hard floor. While she was preparing their makeshift bed, her husband checked the fire in the stove. Watching them, O'Donnell's eyes began to close. Both confused and grateful, he drifted off to sleep, thinking about how they first risked their lives to hide him from the Nazis, and then prepared to sleep on the hard floor so that they could give their bed to a stranger.

O'Donnell woke, before dawn, to find Milka's mother and father sitting next to each other at the long wooden table, drinking coffee from small espresso cups. Her father leaned in and placed his forehead on his wife's, and then he tenderly whispered something in her ear. She smiled, though it didn't quite reach her eyes, and lightly placed her hand on his cheek. Her eyes closed, she placed a light kiss on his lips. When they opened, they glistened from the tears that rolled down her cheeks. Gently wiping her tears away, he continued whispering softly to her.

She lovingly caressed her husband's face. Uncomfortable for intruding, O'Donnell shifted towards the wall. The slight movement caught her eye. She glanced at O'Donnell and quickly wiped the tears from her face. Her husband looked over his broad shoulder, making O'Donnell acutely aware that he had interrupted an intimately emotional moment between husband and wife. Not knowing what else to do, he closed his eyes and pretended to sleep.

At daybreak, they started on another journey. O'Donnell still had no idea as to where they were headed or why, but he assumed they were going to some military camp. Milka's mother, whose name he found out was Andja, cried as she kissed her husband, Slavko, goodbye. She kissed O'Donnell's right cheek, left cheek and then the right cheek again. With a smile she handed him a flask filled with water. Touched at the gesture, O'Donnell bowed his head as he quietly thanked her.

A few of the villagers also gathered to say their goodbyes. The men shook his hand and the women hugged him. The children all clapped and waved, their smiles reaching from ear to ear. O'Donnell was ready to say his farewells to Milka and her family, but was pleasantly surprised as a familiar figure quickly waddled her way over to him. The older woman from yesterday hugged him hard and kissed him three times as well. She cried as she spoke to him. O'Donnell couldn't understand her, but he knew deep down that she was wishing him well.

Finally, Milka and her brothers each said their goodbyes to their father and then to him, each of them bravely holding back their tears. Their inner strength, in fact, the inner strength of everyone in this small village, gave O'Donnell a glimmer of hope that all would eventually end well.

They hiked for several winding miles through the hills of Serbia. Several hours had passed and not a single word was spoken. O'Donnell didn't have the slightest clue as to where they were going, but he wasn't afraid. In fact, after what he experienced the night before, he was confident that Slavko was a good guy. Maybe he was taking him to Tito and the Partisans. He contemplated asking Slavko if they were going to the Partisan camp, but he hesitated. Something in his gut told him just to wait and see.

As they continued their journey, O'Donnell remembered the intimate moment between Slavko and Andja from earlier in the morning. In a way that was difficult to explain, that loving interaction between husband and wife gave the war more meaning than any military briefing ever could. From the air, it was bombs, targets and Nazis. The reality that flesh and blood people were on the ground fighting to keep their families together never really materialized, until now.

Worlds apart, yet so similar. How could he not have realized that the war is so much more than soldiers and politicians? There are real people fighting-good guys versus bad guys. Husbands, wives and children dealing with the very real thought that they would never see each other again. And what kind of people risked their lives and the lives of their children to keep a stranger safe? Slavko and Andja both know the consequences of hiding an American soldier. But they still did. Why?

Thinking about the sacrifice that Slavko and his family were making for him, O'Donnell lost track of time. Lost in his thoughts, he was surprised when Slavko approached another bearded man. Although he was similarly dressed in the khaki pants and shirt, his was more of an actual military uniform. He had a dark green jacket and khaki green pants tucked in to knee high boots that had seen better days. His jacket had medals of honor that no longer shined, but were faded from war. His demeanor, head high, shoulders back and his confident stride, indicated that he wasn't just a soldier, but someone with authority. The soldier greeted O'Donnell with a nod of his head. He and Slavko spoke briefly then the soldier held out his hand to O'Donnell.

"I am Milos. I will take you from here. We must hurry. The Germans are on their patrol and we must make it to the next village before they can find us." At that he turned and shook Slavko's hand. Slavko extended his hand to shake O'Donnell's, then turned and briskly walked back the way they had come.

"You speak English! That's great! My crew and I jumped after our plane was attacked by the Germans yesterday." O'Donnell hesitated. He was so excited to speak to someone who understood him, he forgot that he still wasn't sure if Milos was an ally.

"My name's O'Donnell. I'm an . . ."

"American. I know." Milos interrupted. "We will take you to safety until your men can get you safely out of Yugoslavia."

"If you don't mind me asking, who are 'we'?" O'Donnell felt a surge of confidence from Milos' words. He figured now was as good a time as ever to finally get the answer.

"I am a Major with the Yugoslavian Royal Guard, which is loyal to King Peter. We are now Chetniks, led by General Draza Mihailovich" Milos proclaimed.

O'Donnell was shocked. Chetniks? That didn't make any sense. Why would the Chetniks be helping the Americans? His confidence plummeted. What if this was a set up? The Chetniks were aligned with Hitler, weren't they?

He'd heard about how the Nazis would gather groups of people - men, women and children, and tell them things like they were being taken to safety. The innocent people would be put on a train and sent off to a "safe destination." But instead of safety, those poor people would find themselves in concentration camps and then dead in gas chambers.

"The Germans know about you and your crew. They have been questioning the villagers." Milos paused as he looked backwards over his broad shoulders, scanning the path behind them. He continued, "They will continue to look for all of you, that is why we must hurry. If they find you alive and find out that you have been guarded by Slavko and his family, they will torture and kill them."

"They wouldn't be able to trace me back to them. We're hours away from the village. Not to mention from Slavko and his family." O'Donnell countered. "So at least they should be safe."

"You would be surprised what the Nazis can do. If they don't trace you back to Slavko, they will find any family they can to pay the price of helping their enemy. Do not underestimate what they can do. Their cruelty has no bounds." Milos sped up his pace and continued on the dirt path through the woods.

It was a forested, mountainous area and they were climbing uphill. For being in good physical shape, O'Donnell was embarrassed to realize that he was having a hard time keeping up with Milos. He paused for a minute, hoping that a short rest would rejuvenate him. Milos stopped, albeit reluctantly. With obvious irritation by this temporary stop, he took the flask of water that Andja had given to O'Donnell and handed it to him.

"Drink water. I know the path is a difficult one to travel. However, I must stress again that we must hurry. It is not much farther that we must walk. Take a moment if you have to. But no longer than that." Milos watched O'Donnell as he eagerly drank from the flask.

O'Donnell put the flask back around his neck and nodded to Milos. He didn't want to put anyone in danger. And if what Milos told him was true, someone would be killed if the Germans found him. He did not want that on his conscience.

They walked in silence for another hour. O'Donnell's gut instinct told him that Milos was telling him the truth. If Milos was allied with the Germans, he could have given him up at any moment. Why would Milos take him on this long journey through the wooded mountains just to turn him in? It didn't make any sense.

Contemplating the Chetnik position, O'Donnell was caught off guard when Milos abruptly pushed him behind the bushes that lined the path. "What the . . . ?" Milos quickly put his hand over O'Donnell's mouth. O'Donnell struggled for a few seconds trying to push Milos off of him.

"Be quiet!" he whispered to O'Donnell. "Someone is coming." O'Donnell nodded and Milos let go of his mouth. O'Donnell didn't hear anything. He looked at Milos and was about to question him. Milos shook his head to silence him.

They sat in the bushes for what seemed like an eternity. O'Donnell began questioning Milos' sanity. Paranoia. That's what it was. There wasn't anyone coming and yet they were squatting behind some bushes like scared little rabbits. He was just about to stand up when he heard muffled voices up the path.

A group of four teenage girls were hurriedly walking by, carrying buckets and baskets. A German soldier was following closely behind, watching their every move. The girls were sheet white with fear, but kept walking towards the nearby river. The German laughed and spoke to them, but they ignored him and quickened their pace. The soldier said something again, this time without a trace of humor and they stopped.

With his hand resting on his rifle, he circled them like a wolf circling its prey. He grabbed the basket from the tallest girl in the group, laughing as he continued speaking German to them. She struggled to keep it, but he pulled it from her grasp and started looking through it. Not finding anything of his liking, he tossed it aside. She let go of her friends and ran towards the basket. Upset, she picked it up and shouted at the German. Then to O'Donnell's disbelief, she spit at him! The Nazi lunged forward and grabbed her by the arm. Pulling her forward, he slapped her hard across the face. He was shaking her and shouting. The other girls, afraid to help and afraid to leave their friend, huddled in fear.

Enraged, O'Donnell wanted to jump out of the bushes and shoot the soldier to stop him from hurting the young girl. But Milos put his hand on O'Donnell's arm to stop him. O'Donnell glared at him. There were two of them and they could easily stop this. Milos quickly pulled off his belt and quietly crawled out from behind the bushes. The German, still shouting at the girl, began taunting her. He put his gun to her head and laughed. He pulled the gun away from her and pointed it towards her friends. Terrified, she looked past him and saw Milos crawling towards him on the ground.

The German followed her gaze and spotted Milos. Before he could react, Milos jumped up, kicked the German's gun away and threw the belt around his neck. The German struggled to get the belt off of his neck, but Milos's surprise attack from behind gave him the advantage. The girl ran to her friends as O'Donnell came out from behind the bushes. He grabbed the Nazi's gun, ready to use it if necessary.

After several minutes of struggling, the Nazi collapsed to the ground. Dead. Milos quickly took another flask, filled with plum brandy, and poured it into the German's mouth.

"Quickly, we must drag him to the river and make it look as if he drank too much and then drowned in the river." With that, Milos grabbed the man's legs and dragged him towards the river that was raging not too far away. Confused, O'Donnell ran and picked up the dead German by his arms and the two carried him to the river and threw him in.

They returned to the girls who were tending to their friend.

She wasn't crying anymore. When she saw Milos and O'Donnell, she left her friends and slowly walked up to them.

"*Hvala*" She said quietly as tears streamed down her face. O'Donnell had heard the word enough to figure it meant "Thank you." He nodded and said, "You're welcome." Milos asked her some things in Serbian. She shook her head side to side. Milos briskly checked her arms and her face. Her left eye had swollen to the size of a golf ball and had turned a dark shade of blue and black from the bruising. He instructed her and her friends to go back home and to stay there, as it was the safest place for them.

They thanked the men again, quickly grabbed their baskets and buckets, and ran back the way they had come.

"Why did you let it get that far?" O'Donnell demanded. "We could have just shot that jerk dead and he wouldn't have had a chance to bruise up that poor girl like that."

"Yes, we could have shot him." Milos agreed. "But that shot would have been heard for miles."

"So what, the Nazi's would have found me? Or maybe not. We could have hidden from them. But at least that girl wouldn't have been beaten. We could have saved her from that.

"You purposely let her get roughed up, didn't you?"

Milos continued searching the ground for signs of struggle. Satisfied, he looked up at O'Donnell and smirked.

O'Donnell's adrenaline was still running high. The Serb's smirk pushed him over the edge. He pushed Milos as he continued, "You did! You ass! What they say about you Chetniks is true. You are sick."

Caught off guard by the shove, Milos stumbled back and fell.

Angry now himself, Milos jumped to his feet and pushed O'Donnell back. Nose to nose, Milos replied, "If that is what you and your Americans think, so be it. But if we had alerted the other Germans, they would have come. They might not have found us, but they might have found those girls.

"And if they found one of their own dead, especially from a gunshot wound, they would not only have killed the girls. But they would have gone into their village and killed ninety-six more innocent Serbians there. For every German soldier that is killed, they kill one hundred Serbians. Not soldiers, but ANY men, women and children." Milos pushed O'Donnell away in disgust.

"We are not the *Partisans*." Milos spat out as he continued. "We don't kill the Germans without any care or thought to the consequence to our own people. We don't sacrifice our people for political advancement." Milos paused and looked O'Donnell squarely in the eye.

"The Partisans kill Germans, knowing that the Germans retaliation is extreme and many more Serbs would die. They don't care. They are more concerned with establishing Communism in our country and killing as many Chetniks as they can." He paused for a moment to gather his thoughts. He stepped back, never looking away from O'Donnell. With a combination of pride and weariness, he continued.

"The Germans are our common enemy. They have taken over our country and are terrorizing our people. We fight them in battles, and we will continue to fight until we have our country back and every vicious Nazi is off our land.

"We also attack the Germans, but in ways that try to preserve innocent Serbian lives from unnecessary death or torture from German retaliation. We are strategic. We are guerilla fighters and we use sabotage when we can to defeat them. When necessary we attack with all out war. But we try to defeat the enemy with minimal loss of Serbian lives in the process. That is the difference between us and those Partisans you have chosen as your allies." Milos put his belt back on and fastened it.

"You may not understand or agree with our ways. But shooting that one German would have cost the lives of one hundred innocent girls like the ones we just saw. You may think I acted cowardly. But I did what was necessary for an entire village to survive." With that, Milos turned and walked away. He stopped and turned back towards O'Donnell.

"We need to make it to the next village before dark. If we are going to do that, we must leave now. You can continue with me or you can go on your own, the choice is yours. But I would recommend coming with me. We are your only true allies here."

Unsure of anything anymore, O'Donnell hedged his bets and followed Milos.

CHAPTER 8

THE COOL EARLY summer night air swirled around Petrovich as he sat outside, absently staring into space. Base activity never fully ceased, but at this time of night it was minimal. Shutting his eyes, he leaned his head back against the wall and shoved his hands into his coat pockets to keep warm. Frustration and anger surged through him as he thought about O'Donnell.

Two weeks had passed and they still hadn't heard from him. At least that was the "official" story. But Petrovich didn't buy it. Not just because all of his instincts screamed that O'Donnell was alive, nor because he knew O'Donnell was one of their best. But because he overheard one of the OSS Agents, Captain George Vujnovich, arguing with a British SOE agent. And Petrovich later confirmed the story through his own contacts on base.

Evidently, there had been some transmissions coming in from Yugoslavia for the past several months from the fliers that had been shot down over the that time frame. But the British SOE agents were adamant that the transmissions were to be ignored. They were "confident" that the transmissions were Chetnik attempts to sabotage the Allies. But Captain Vujnovich disagreed.

The transmissions were coming from General Mihailovich

and they were reporting that they had rescued several downed American airmen in Serbia. He was urging that arrangements be made to evacuate them by air. The British continued to ignore the requests.

Petrovich's gut told him that those transmissions should be taken seriously and not ignored. They should find out for certain if there were men behind enemy lines. But there always seemed to be some SOE agents that were quick to dismiss any positive information about the Chetnik side. Like they had their own hidden agenda. Whatever that could be. Petrovich shook his head. He was becoming paranoid like them, second-guessing even his own allies on base.

The SOE's position was painstakingly clear. Per British officials, if there were Allied men on the ground in Yugoslavia, the Chetniks were handing them over to the Nazis. And they didn't believe there were as many Allied men on the ground as the Chetniks claimed.

They were determined that the transmissions, that were coming in suspiciously uncoded, were a Chetnik ploy to ambush the Allies if they went in for a rescue.

Regardless, Petrovich couldn't understand how they could so easily dismiss the Chetnik claims. Those were American men, for God's sake! And Vujnovich had enough intelligence through the OSS to be confident that the Chetniks were not planning an ambush.

In fact, Vujnovich and Captain George Musulin, another OSS Agent that had spent time in Yugoslavia with General Mihailovich, were just as adamant that the transmissions were real, and that there were downed airmen in Serbia, Yugoslavia. And that Mihailovich had rescued them and wanted to evacuate them. They were working on trying to get permission to go in and see for themselves. And that wasn't going well, at all.

Petrovich opened his eyes, took his hands out of his pockets, rubbed them together and blew warm air into them. Getting up, he stretched his hands high above his head. As he did, he saw a star shoot across the sky. At that exact moment, he decided he wouldn't sit around any more. He was going to get some answers. And no one was going to stop him.

The next morning, Petrovich made a point to look for the one person who always seemed to know everything that was going on, regardless if it was public knowledge or not. He didn't care if he didn't particularly like Red. Sometimes you took one for the team. This was one of those times.

He found Red sitting with a group of British fliers and a few of their SOE agents. They were sitting around a table eating breakfast and talking. They didn't have any flights going out this morning, so they were blowing off some steam.

Petrovich approached them casually, not wanting to look too eager. He couldn't say why, but his instincts were always on high alert around Red and these men. But he needed reliable information and he didn't want to give them any reason to hold back.

"Mornin' men" Petrovich said as he with an exaggerated yawn.

"Goodness, Petrovich!" Red laughed, "you could swallow us whole with that enormous yawn! Not much sleep last night, I take it."

"Nope. I tossed and turned all night. Having a hard time taking it in that O'Donnell hasn't been in contact with us." Petrovich looked away then added, "Just feels like we are deserting him and the others."

Red glanced quickly at the SOE agent across from him. It was just a flicker, so fast that Petrovich almost missed it. Almost. So there was something there. Now he just had to figure out what that something was.

"That sounds quite accusatory. We don't even know if he is

alive. And if he is, where he might be. Can't desert someone if we don't have a bloody clue of his whereabouts or even if he is still amongst the living." Red kept his eyes on Petrovich as he sipped his tea. "Unless you've heard something to the contrary?"

"Word around base is that there have been transmissions coming in from Yugoslavia - from Mihailovich's camp. That he's rescued some of our men and wants to arrange an air evacuation. Do you know anything about it?" Petrovich asked Red, but looked at the SOE agent as he asked. The agent's gaze didn't waiver from Petrovich. But the slight tick in his jaw gave him away.

"That's rubbish for sure. Mihailovich is not our friend. If he has our men, he's surely turning them over to the Germans." Red shook his head, looked into his coffee cup and then continued, "As for arranging an evacuation, that would be suicide for anyone of us. They'd certainly ambush us."

"I don't know. How does that make any sense? What's the point of ambushing one plane's crew?" Petrovich contemplated out loud. They knew something. He was sure of it. "Not sure that's it."

"Petrovich, it's quite honorable of you to be so devoted to your friend and hold on to hope that he's alive and well with Mihailovic. We all hope he is alive. But the reality is that if the Chetniks were arranging a legitimate evacuation of Allied men, they would be coding their transmissions" the SOE agent with the tick interjected. "Any successful rescue would have to be through Tito, and only Tito. Mihailovich is our enemy."

Red and the others all nodded in agreement. Petrovich hadn't mentioned the uncoded transmissions and he wasn't about to point that out. Now he was absolutely sure that they knew more than what they were letting on.

"True. I guess. But I've heard some of our OSS agents say

otherwise. How can you be so sure that Tito has our men and Mihailovich doesn't?"

"Those OSS agents you are referring to are irritatingly persistent on their quest to go to Mihailovich's camp. Quite irritating, in fact. They are dead set on dropping in to his camp to verify for themselves whether or not he has them. They are insane for even thinking such rubbish. They would be walking into their own death traps."

"Maybe. But what if they aren't crazy? What if they have enough intelligence that says that the transmissions are true? Why aren't we going in to see? Shouldn't we be doing everything in our power to rescue our men? And if Tito has them, why hasn't he contacted us too? Something just doesn't make sense."

The SOE agent's tick returned at Petrovich's last group of questions. Petrovich watched as the agent looked at the men seated around the table, pause briefly on Red, then look Petrovich directly in the eye.

"Lieutenant Petrovich, Tito is our ally in Yugoslavia. All of OUR intelligence suggests nothing to the contrary. We will not forsake our one and only ally in a volatile region such as Yugoslavia to proceed on a wild goose chase with our enemies.

"Yugoslavia is a hotbed of violent activity as we speak. In Croatia and Bosnia, there are the Ustasha who are viciously torturing and killing Serbs, Jews, and Gypsies by the hundreds of thousands. They are devoted to the Nazi/Fascist cause to a chilling extreme. Their agenda? An independent state of Croatia that is free of these three particular groups of people that they deem dirty and unworthy of life." He shuddered as he paused.

"At times our intelligence tells us that they are WORSE than the Nazis! They are vicious monsters, skinning people alive, gouging out their eyes and other forms of sheer torture. And they are fulfilling their goal of eradicating the Serbs, Jews and

Gypsies to a chillingly accurate degree. Thanks to Hitler himself, they finally have their own country and they will do anything to keep it.

"The Chetniks are fighting Tito and the Ustasha. The Ustasha are fighting the Chetniks. But Tito is the only one who is also fighting the Germans and the Italians. He is our only hope in that region. The rest can fight each other all day and night. They can kill each other off as far as we are concerned. Because if they fight each other, then, Tito can focus on helping us fight and defeat the Germans, win the war and free Yugoslavia."

"Don't be a fool, Petrovich." Red added. "If Mihailovich has any of our men, they are doomed. And so would be anyone who would go in and try to arrange an evacuation plan with him. We just need to wait and when the time is right, go in and work with Tito to free any captured men. Sorry, my friend, but that is the reality of the situation. It is, as they say, the cold, hard truth. If O'Donnell is there, his only hope is Tito."

O'Donnell's heart raced as he realized that they had no intention of supporting any rescue mission. They were perfectly fine ignoring the calls for help from their own men in Yugoslavia, just because they came from the other camp. He struggled to keep his voice calm.

"I appreciate what you're all telling me. But where I come from, you don't just sit and wait for things to be easy before you go after what you want. If Mihailovich says he has them, then I strongly believe that we shouldn't just ignore it and wait for Tito." He picked up Red's tea and drank. Looking Red in the eye, he set the cup down.

"From the looks of it, I'd say that Tito is your man. But from my perspective, anyone who is willing to save a friend or two of mine from the hands of the Nazis is my man. Regardless of whether he is a Partisan or a Chetnik. You ever think your intelligence just might be wrong?" he asked the SOE agent.

"No, I don't, Lieutenant. I trust my colleagues in the field. To survive this war, we truly have no choice. Do we?"

"I guess not. But I've also learned that people can be duped and people make mistakes. And the one and only solid thing I can count on in every situation is my gut." Placing his hands on the table he leaned in close to Red. "And my gut tells me that O'Donnell is safe. And that he isn't with Tito, that he is with Mihailovich. That's enough for me. " With that, he got up and walked out of the building.

He slipped on his jacket and sunglasses as he closed the door behind him. They may want to wait for their buddy Tito to make a move. But Petrovich wasn't waiting around for that. They knew something and they weren't talking. He was more determined than ever to find a way to get someone to arrange that forsaken evacuation. And there wasn't any time to lose.

CHAPTER 9

THEY WALKED FOR weeks, only stopping to sleep in tiny villages ripped apart by war. The villagers were amazing, O'Donnell admitted to himself. Despite the devastation they'd endured, they made a point to go out of their way to greet him, make him comfortable, and feed him. Then to top it all off, they'd do generous things like give up their beds to give him a soft place to sleep. The kindness was never ending.

They were enduring heart-wrenching struggles. Even with barely enough food to feed themselves, they were still adamant about feeding him first. Just like Milka and her family, they would only eat after they felt that he had enough, and that usually meant scraps for their families.

The war had turned their lives upside down - again. World War I had demolished their country. The death and destruction were enormous-so was the bitter hatred for the Germans because of it. They had just begun to rebuild their lives, to move forward with their families. Then Hitler decided to plow through and essentially take over their country-without their permission. They refused to let him take it without a fight. And boy, were they fighting!

According to Milos, from the very beginning, when Hitler tried to force young King Peter into a pact, a wave of rebellion flowed through the countryside. People were rioting and shouting, *"Bolje rat nego pakt! Bolje grob nego rob!"* (A war is better than the pact! Better to be in the grave than to be their slave!) And they vowed to fight until the very last man.

"The Balkans," Milos boasted, "have a history of war." He wasn't proud of the wars, but he was proud of the way his ancestors had reacted during those wars. Honor was a word he used often in his descriptions. And then there was the Battle of Kosovo.

"Over five hundred years ago," Milos explained, "in June of 1389, the battle for Kosovo took place between the Christian Serbs and the Islamic Ottoman Turks. Legend has it that Serbian Czar Lazar was visited by an Angel the night before the battle and presented the Czar with a choice. He could forfeit the battle and submit to the Turks for a Kingdom on Earth. Or fight the Turks and be assured a reward in the Kingdom of Heaven.

"Knowing the odds were stacked against them, the Turks greatly outnumbered us and they had more and better weapons, Czar Lazar chose his fate.

"The next day, he told his men the choice that was presented to them. His soldiers chose honor. They all stepped forward to fight for what was theirs, for what was right, and die for it if necessary. The Czar and his soldiers were blessed by the Serbian Orthodox priests, took their final communion and went off into battle."

Milos paused to drink from his flask. His face showed an odd combination of sadness and pride as he continued.

"They fought hard and gave their all, but they lost. Over seventy-seven thousand Serbian soldiers died that day in the Field of Blackbirds in Kosovo. It was one of the bloodiest days in their history and one of their proudest. Proudest because they fought, despite the certainty that they would all die in battle. They did not surrender and they died honorably.

"The battle was so ruthless that the green grassy field turned a deep shade of red from all of the blood. God rest their souls," Milos said as he crossed himself. "And each year, thousands of roses, the color of blood, bloom across the ancient battlefield. A reminder from God of the sacrifice our ancestors made for Him."

"But they lost." O'Donnell thought of the Alamo. Similar outcomes, similar pride to never forget. "What happened to the survivors?"

"They became slaves of the Ottoman Empire for five hundred years. It was a tragic era in our history. One in which we stubbornly held onto our identity and our faith in God. But it was not easy.

"In Bosnia, for example, the Turks systematically took all of the first-born Serbian boys from their families and raised them in Turkey. Then they changed the boys' names to sound Islamic and taught them Islam. They returned them to Bosnia as strangers to their own mothers, fathers, and faith." He paused as he looked at O'Donnell.

"Imagine the pain in the mother's heart at not even being able to recognize her own son. But by the Grace of God, we have been free of the Turks for over a century. And during the time of Ottoman occupation, we refused to allow our identity or our faith to succumb to them. We prayed to God and honored our saints in secrecy. And we NEVER forgot Kosovo. It is that spirit of Kosovo that keeps Serbian people alive. It is what keeps us fighting today."

O'Donnell pretended to understand, but the reality was that he couldn't fully understand the plight of these people because he had never had to fight for those things. As an American, he had always been blessed with the ability to choose and live free of these kinds of fears. It was something he took for granted, but he realized now that those freedoms that he had were precious.

He didn't think he would ever take even the simplest things for granted anymore.

"We will be stopping shortly. There you will find many more soldiers such as yourself." Milos interrupted his thoughts. "We will stay there."

"How many other soldiers are there?"

"Many. Just as we have found you, we have been finding Americans and other Allied soldiers across the country for months. We have been gathering them and keeping them safe, until they can be evacuated."

"Has anyone made contact with our guys? Do they even know you have us?"

"Yes."

"Where . . . when is the evacuation?" O'Donnell asked excited at the prospect of being rescued.

"There isn't one. They refuse to come."

"What do you mean they refuse to come?" Stunned, O'Donnell gaped at Milos.

"General Mihailovic has been sending messages letting them know that many have been rescued and that he would like to arrange an evacuation. But they have not responded."

Were the allies getting the messages? O'Donnell guessed they probably were. It ate him straight to the gut, but he knew why they weren't responding. They didn't like Mihailovic. And probably didn't believe him.

How many times did they emphasize to look for Tito's Partisans? Heck, they painted Mihailovic and his Chetniks as a group of rugged monsters that would torture and kill any Allied soldier without batting an eye. They thought it was a set up. There would be no other reason to ignore the transmissions.

It might be too early to tell, but from all of the people he had met, including Slavko and Milos, he wondered how the Allies could have had it so wrong? These men weren't monsters. They'd fed him and kept him safe and as comfortable as they could. An enemy, especially cold-blooded killers, wouldn't go to those lengths. And according to Milos, and from what O'Donnell has seen with his own eyes, they considered the Germans the enemy. And they would fight the Germans until the last man.

"Do not worry. General Mihailovic has not given up. He will continue to try and make contact until he can evacuate you and your fellow soldiers. He is a great man of honor and a man of his word. If he has committed to getting you all out of Yugoslavia safely, then you can be sure that he will not rest until he has done it."

O'Donnell didn't know what to say. Their country was being torn apart on so many different levels, so he couldn't understand how a man with so much responsibility for his own people could place such an emphasis on rescuing the very men who considered him an enemy.

The pre-dusk sky was a kaleidoscope of colors. The light cascaded through the thick forest of trees, creating a show of lights as the trees swayed in the light breeze. In the distance, O'Donnell could hear the explosions and gunfire from the battle raging nearby. It was almost comical to him that it could be so peaceful here and yet a war was being fought all around him.

It was a beautiful country. Green mountains took over the horizon, while deep forests and long grassy fields interchanged along the landscape. The simple villages completed the countryside with their concrete walls and tiled roof homes that were surrounded by farmland that was worked by the villagers.

Tragically, they had passed through several villages that no longer held that simple charm. Instead, they were now charred remains of buildings and farmland as the Germans, or Croatian Ustasha, attacked and wreaked devastation. Their enemies were vicious and showed no mercy.

"We will be arriving shortly."

"OK. Where to after this stop? And is anyone going with us?"

"This is our last stop, Pranjane. That is where we have been hiding most of the American airmen. We hope this is the place from where you will eventually be rescued," Milos answered.

O'Donnell's hopes were rising, but only slightly. If they couldn't convince the Allies that Mihailovich's claims were legitimate, they might be stuck here until the war ended, or worse, until the Nazis found them.

O'Donnell looked towards the sky and made a silent plea to his friend, Jack. *Buddy, if there were any time I could use a helping hand from you, this would be it. Not sure what you can do, but if you can get our guys in Italy to believe Mihailovich, I'd be forever grateful.* He didn't want to stay in Yugoslavia until the end of the war, and he definitely didn't want to think about what the Nazis would do if they found him. All he could do was pray.

O'Donnell and Milos entered camp a short while later. When they got there, O'Donnell was dumbfounded. He'd seriously underestimated the number of soldiers he would find in Pranjane. When Milos said many, O'Donnell thought twenty or thirty. What he found was incredible! Not twenty or thirty, instead, it was hundreds of soldiers, mostly American!

Seeing O'Donnell's shock, Milos explained that Mihailovich and his men had been rescuing the Allies for several months, from all over Yugoslavia. As the Chetniks found the men, they hid them from the Nazis, just as they hid O'Donnell. O'Donnell couldn't fathom how they did it. To hide this many men from the Germans and still manage to fight the war around them, it was truly amazing.

Hoping to find someone from his crew, O'Donnell slowly scanned the groups of people. He recognized several of the men, but not one from his crew. Damn. He didn't want to think what could have happened to them. He just hoped that they might have been rescued and were on their way with a different group of Chetniks.

"Hey! O'Donnell?" shouted an American soldier, sitting across camp at a wooden table with a few other soldiers that O'Donnell didn't recognize.

He walked over to the group, excited to have a fellow American to talk to. At first, he couldn't recognize the soldier, whose face was covered by a full-grown bushy black beard. But as he got closer, he realized it was Staff Sergeant Mike Wallace. He didn't know Sergeant Wallace very well, but they'd spoken a few times on base.

"Sergeant Wallace." O'Donnell saluted. "It's a relief to see you, sir."

"At ease, Lieutenant. We're pretty lax on formalities at this point." Sergeant Wallace smiled. "Welcome to Pranjane."

"I have to be honest, I think I am happy to be here."

Sergeant Wallace burst out with a deep laugh. "Son, this is the best place to be, outside of Allied territory. As long as we continue to stay under the German radar, we are safe here. These guys," he gestured to the four other bearded men sitting around the table, as well to those walking around the camp, "well, they've pretty much committed to keeping us safe until we get back home."

O'Donnell looked at the men. They weren't Allied soldiers. In fact, they were a formidable sight. Although they were sitting, O'Donnell could tell that the men were all very tall, probably at least six feet or more. They were wearing black wool hats with pins attached to the front. The pins were bearing the Royal Insignia of a two headed crowned eagle with a crest that had four C's, backs facing each other, surrounding a cross.

"Sit! Drink!" said one of the men as he poured a small glass of the local favorite, plum brandy.

O'Donnell sat down and joined the men. He swallowed a

large sip of the strong brandy. Squinting his eyes as the whiskey burned its way down his throat, he shook his head and started coughing. The Serbian soldier laughed and good-naturedly slapped him on the back.

"Good? Yes?" he asked.

"Yes!" O'Donnell choked.

"How long have you been on the ground?" asked Sergeant Wallace.

"A few weeks. We've been traveling by foot through the mountainside, stopping in the local villages to sleep and eat. How about you and the rest of the men?"

"Most of us have been here for several months. I've been downed just over three. It's been a long three months and I'm about ready to get back." He paused as he drank some of his plum brandy. He was tapping his fingers on the table as he looked fondly at the men seated at the table.

"That's not to say that these guys haven't gone out of their way to feed us and keep us safe. They have. In fact, outside of the fact that we are in the middle of a forsaken war, they've been mighty hospitable. But, I'd feel a lot better not being surrounded by the Nazis.

"What these people are doing for us is amazing. It's crazy that our guys think they're the enemy."

"I'm having a hard time with that too. They're nothing like the monsters they were made out to be. I practically jumped into the hands of the Germans as my plane went down. But these guys got me first. What happened to you?"

"Yeah, most of us have similar stories as to how we got here. Mine? Well, like you, we crash landed. A few of our guys were trapped in the plane. We tried to get them out, when a German patrol came by. Before the Nazis could capture us, a group of Chetniks came out of nowhere and held them off until we freed our men."

Sergeant Wallace pointed to the man sitting across the table. He was young, barely sixteen. He stared at O'Donnell for a moment before he looked at Wallace. A small pride-filled smirk slowly emerged across his face as Wallace continued his story.

"Branko, here? He came out of the trees like a damn monkey, firing his rifle and surprised the heck out of those Germans. The Nazis didn't see him nor the rest of them coming.

"The fighting was brutal. And the Chetniks suffered tremendous casualties that day, just to save us. It's humbling to think of what they sacrificed. But they freed our men and got us out of there. And they've been by our side ever since."

O'Donnell listened as Sergeant Wallace told him how even the peasants refused to tell the Nazis where the Americans were. The Nazis knew how many they were hiding, because they counted the parachutes as they came down. But the peasants wouldn't turn over the Americans. And because they didn't, the Nazis executed one peasant hostage, including women and children, for each American parachute they saw. The warning was clear: if they continued to hide the Allied airmen, they would execute that many more peasants until they were found. Regardless, the peasants still wouldn't turn in the Americans.

"I witnessed Nazi brutality and what they're capable of. But I didn't see anything like that," said O'Donnell. "It's sick. They have no regard for human life."

"I have no way of understanding the way the Nazis think. I just know we have to do whatever we can to stop them. And in the meantime, figure out a way to get out of here, so we can stop them once and for all."

"How the heck are we going to do that, when Mihailovich's messages aren't getting through?" Looking over his shoulder, then at the men at the table, O'Donnell lowered his voice to a whisper, "And you know our guys are getting them. They're just ignoring them because they don't trust him. How are we going to get them to realize that he isn't the enemy?"

"We've got some guys working on it with Mihailovic. Let's hope their idea works." Wallace replied as he stood up. "In the meantime, we have a debt to repay. If you're up to it, come with us and let's take down some Nazis."

CHAPTER 10

WALLACE, O'DONNELL AND Branko ventured into the forest along with several other Serb and American soldiers. Scattered into small groups of two to three men each, they carried grenades, ammunition and rifles that they carefully hid beneath their clothing.

The Nazis relied heavily on the local trains to transport ammunition and fuel to their troops throughout Yugoslavia and the rest of Europe. As luck would have it, there was a train stopped nearby that was unloading supplies to the Nazis and it would be leaving the station shortly.

"There's the station," whispered Wallace. On cue, Branko slipped ahead of the groups and continued alone towards the station. The others spread out and hid in the trees and bushes. O'Donnell was amazed. Barely sixteen, and Branko was taking the lead on this mission.

Up above on the grassy and forested hill, they had a direct view of the station below. O'Donnell glanced at Wallace who was crouched next to him, keeping Branko in his view at all times.

"Stay down, O'Donnell. The element of surprise is our best offense. And you can't get better at guerilla warfare than these guys. Just watch," Wallace whispered.

Two Nazis casually patrolled the train and the station. They paused at the far end of the train to light their cigarettes. One leaned against a train car and lifted his head and exhaled the cigarette smoke while the other one crouched on the ground. They erupted in laughter at the obvious joke that passed between them. Realizing that he caught them at the right moment, Branko snuck around to the other side of the train and climbed to the top of the engine.

He lifted himself up and over into the car, careful to make as little noise as possible, then peeked over the top to make sure that they were still at the other end of the train. They were still taking their break, so Branko opened his bag and pulled out a grenade. But instead of pulling the pin and throwing it, he dug through the coal and hid the grenade about a third of the way down.

The Nazis threw their cigarette butts on the ground and started their leisurely walk back. They were still laughing from whatever story they had started earlier. Branko peeked over the top and saw that they were one car away. He quickly crawled out of the car and down the side and jumped onto the ground.

The Nazis stopped abruptly. Branko froze. He placed his hand on the rifle strapped across his back and slowly brought it forward. He held his breath and waited to see what they would do next.

O'Donnell watched in horror as the Nazis suddenly stopped their slow walk back up the train line. He needed to create a diversion to give the kid a chance to get away. He tried to get up. But before he could move, Wallace raised his hand, shook his head and nodded toward the train. Not sure he completely understood, O'Donnell mouthed "Why?"

"Wait," was all Wallace whispered.

The Nazis leaned in close to each other and pointed at the

train. They crept forward and kneeled down to look underneath the car. Branko was a dead man if they found him. Ready to pounce, O'Donnell's chest throbbed with the anxious beating of his heart.

Apparently unsatisfied, the Germans separated, one moving forward and the other going back the way they came. Branko hung upside down, his knees wrapped over the rungs of the ladder on the side of the car. He peeked underneath the train and watched them go in opposite directions. Taking his chances, he pulled himself up and quietly climbed to the ground.

He bolted into the woods. Just as he disappeared behind the trees, the Nazis rounded to the other side of the train. Not seeing anything out of the ordinary, they continued their patrol, business as usual.

O'Donnell, Wallace and the others left their post and retreated back towards camp. O'Donnell scanned the hills for any sign of Branko.

"What about the kid?"

"He'll be fine. This is what they do best," Wallace replied.

"I thought we were going to take them down. Branko didn't get to finish what he started."

"The intention wasn't to battle it out with them in an outright gunfight. Nor to blow up the train . . . right now. That would cause a backlash onto the local peasants. We need to avoid that as much as possible. This was better.

"Branko put that grenade deep into the pile of coal. When the train leaves to its next destination, with the Nazi's and their supplies on it, they're going to have a big surprise about ten minutes into their trip! Because when they shovel that pile of coal into the engine . . ."

"The grenade will explode in the engine! And the train and the Nazis with it!" O'Donnell finished for Wallace.

"But the beauty of it is that they won't know who did it or how exactly it happened. So they won't punish the locals. But we accomplish our goal. The Chetniks do it all the time. Sabotage. Guerilla warfare. It's the only way they can have any chance of winning this war."

They continued their walk through the mountainside. Forests of thick trees spread across the mountain, with fields of tall green grass interspersed between. A few feet away, a fast flowing stream swooshed as it flowed over the occasional pile of rocks or wood.

"They know this land like the backs of their hands" Wallace continued. "They know every cave, hill, nook, river, and hole. The element of surprise is theirs. They aren't armed as well as the enemy. But that doesn't matter. They have home turf advantage. Which is why Hitler has had to deploy so many divisions just to try and keep Yugoslavia occupied. It's really brilliant on the part of Mihailovich and his men."

"It feels great to be back to business! But I'll feel a lot better when I see Branko back at camp."

Grinning, Wallace winked at O'Donnell. "He'll be there!"

About a half a mile outside of camp, O'Donnell saw a huge cloud of black smoke billowing in the western sky. He covered his mouth and nose to stop from gagging from the horrendous stench that filled the air.

"That's disgusting! What the heck is burning?" he shouted.

"I hope it's not what I think it is," Wallace replied as he took off running up the hill. From the top of the hill, Milos jogged towards Wallace and O'Donnell.

"Milos, what's going on?" O'Donnell asked.

"The Germans demanded that we turn over the Americans. General Mihailovic refused," Milos replied as he adjusted his rifle across his chest. "The Germans threatened to burn the entire village to the ground if we didn't comply with their demands." He paused for a moment as he looked towards the sky, an unspoken prayer on his lips. He tried to hide the sorrow in his eyes, but he couldn't.

"What? Are you serious? Is that what happened over there?" O'Donnell shouted as he bolted towards the top of the hill. "Are you people crazy? You just let them . . . ." He stopped in his tracks at the top. On the other side of the hill, he saw a dozen or so small houses still smoldering from the fire. Crops were burned to the ground. But worse, much worse, the charred remains of innocent people, some obviously women, children and elderly, lay scattered throughout the village.

O'Donnell fell to his knees. He covered his face to hide the horrific scene that would forever be burned into his memory. Tears streamed down his face as he cried for those innocent Serbian villagers, sacrificed for him and all of the rescued Allied men. At the thought of the children, his stomach rolled and he started to vomit.

Wallace and Milos waited a few feet away. They understood the revulsion, confusion, and anger he felt. Unfortunately, they had seen this and other atrocities too many times before. The Nazis and Ustasha were merciless in their attacks.

O'Donnell put his hands on his knees but kept his head down. He couldn't look at the blackened village, nor could he look at Milos.

After several minutes, he slowly rose to his feet. Still looking down, his voice was hoarse. "You should have turned us in. We would have figured something out. That's what we've been trained for. Those poor innocent people . . . they didn't . . . DIDN'T . . . deserve this. Especially because of us."

"O'Donnell, I know it's hard for you to understand. It's hard for me too, answered Wallace. "As Americans, we've never had to make choices like this. Makes us realize how much we take for granted. But these are the choices they're forced to make, not just today or during this war. They've been making these kinds of sacrifices for centuries."

"But why not give us up instead of your own people? Why?" he shouted at Milos.

"We could have turned you and your men over to them," Milos replied. "They would have either killed all of you or kept you as prisoners of war. Then they would have torched the village anyway, to punish us for hiding you and to warn others to not to make the same mistake."

"You don't know that."

"Yes, I do. Our lives are meaningless to them. The only hope our people have is to return you safe so that you can help us beat them. Sabotage and guerilla warfare will only take us so far."

"But those people . . ." O'Donnell choked.

"May God have mercy on their souls and may their memories be eternal. Their sacrifice will never be forgotten," Milos answered as he crossed himself and walked ahead of them towards camp.

O'Donnell's heart ached with the knowledge that those people were killed, no not just killed, but tortured, burned to death, just to keep him and the other Americans safe. How could he live with that? As if reading his thoughts, Wallace placed his hand on O'Donnell's shoulder.

"I know it's hard to grasp. I hate it too. But the Nazis would have done it anyway. They've done it before. In the town of Kraljevo, they went to the local school and lined up all of the children and teachers. The children ranged in age from six to eighteen. After they were all lined up, the Germans stood in front of them, raised their machine guns, and executed each and every one of them."

"Oh my God. Why?" O'Donnell asked in horror.

"In retaliation for the death of ONE of their soldiers. For every one of their soldiers killed, they kill one hundred Serbs, including women and children." Wallace gestured towards the charred village. "This is what happens all across this God-forsaken country. Why the hell do you think they want us to win this war?"

CHAPTER 11

WHOSE SIDE ARE these Brits on anyway? Petrovich wondered as he replayed his most recent conversation with Red.

"Mihailovich can't be trusted. That was plain as day as he disobeyed British orders to destroy the two bridges on the Ibar and Morava rivers. It was made perfectly clear to him that those railways needed to be disrupted to prevent the Nazis from using them," Red argued.

"But he DID destroy those bridges!" Petrovich argued back. "Just because he didn't destroy them at the specific points London designated doesn't mean he failed at the mission. Or that he disobeyed. The end result was still the same!"

"Why do you think he chose different points? Isn't it obvious?"

"Are you serious? Red, the bridges were destroyed. The Nazis couldn't get through. We both know damn well that if he would have used the points London chose, he would have stranded thousands of people in Bosnia, which, by the way, were mostly women and children. They would have been sitting ducks for the Nazis. No doubt slaughtered and tortured too."

"That's what Mihailovich claims. Our intelligence thinks otherwise. Mihailovich is a nuisance."

"If I didn't know better," Petrovich stepped closer to Red and looked down at him, "I'd think that you tried and convicted Mihailovic before the war even began. Why are you so gung-ho for that commie and hell bent against Mihailovich?"

Red raised his eyebrow in just the slightest way, but enough to show Petrovich that the word "commie" struck a chord with Red.

"Petrovich, you have a vivid imagination, that is quite evident. Regardless of what you or I think of Tito's political views, he is our ally. And Mihailovich is our enemy. It seems that, unlike you, I respect the judgment of my superiors in London and don't question their authority. You would be wise to do the same for Washington."

"Oh, I listen to my guys back in D.C. Don't you think otherwise. It's your guys that I'm questioning. Tell me this. Mihailovich destroyed those bridges AND saved thousands of innocent people. What hurts Churchill more?" He paused as he leaned within inches of Red's face. "The fact that he disobeyed the almighty Churchill? Or that Mihailovich's way was better?"

"I won't even dignify that with a response," Red shot back, stumbling backwards.

"Of course not. Because if you did, you'd have to admit that Mihailovich isn't the enemy your guys want him to be."

Red stalked off towards the bunkhouses. Petrovich watched as he stopped to speak to a group of men that Petrovich was sure were both OSS and SOE agents. They were gathered in front of the bunkhouse, listening to Red. An agent would occasionally look over Red's shoulder, make eye contact with Petrovich, and then revert his attention back to Red. Petrovich had no doubt what they were talking about.

Suddenly, they dispersed. Some went into the bunkhouse, others left with Red. Where were they going? Petrovich decided to give them a small head start before following them. Red was a bit too Tito friendly for Petrovich.

Petrovich followed closely behind, careful to duck behind walls to avoid their watchful eyes as they occasionally glanced over their shoulders. Eventually, they found a table at the far end of the base and sat. Petrovich doubled back around the building and snuck towards the corner, just within earshot. He leaned against the wall, put his hands in his pockets, and listened.

Fifteen minutes passed with nothing but random chitchat. Petrovich had his fill of nonsense and gave up. Maybe he was paranoid, after all. Feeling ridiculous he pushed himself away from the wall and started to walk away. As if on cue, the conversation turned. Petrovich stopped and leaned towards the edge of the corner and listened.

"Vujnovich has been trying to get Roosevelt to approve a rescue mission in Yugoslavia. Seems that he is convinced that Mihailovich is telling the truth." said an OSS agent.

"He is the last person we would want to go there. Who knows the extent he would take to sabotage our efforts. He has made it clear that he is against our cause." replied one of the SOE agents.

Red lowered his voice. "This could cause a major problem. It's imperative that we do whatever is necessary to prevent any assistance from reaching Mihailovic."

The OSS agent explained that Vujnovich, a fellow OSS agent, had been diligent in trying to overcome the barriers to going into Mihailovich's camp. Vujnovich felt that the real reason that Mihailovich's pleas were being ignored was that if they did go in, and actually found the rescued airmen, the British and the Americans would have to eat crow. How could the Chetniks be Nazi collaborators while at the same time rescuing Allied Airmen and keeping them safe from the Nazis?

Petrovich considered this new piece of information. His gut never let him down in the past, and again it was right on target.

"He could ruin everything if he succeeds. We cannot allow that to happen. Is Klugman aware of this? He could use his connections to prevent Vujnovich from getting his way on this." Red responded.

James Klugman? Petrovich was now convinced that the SOE was infiltrated with communist moles. Petrovich had never met Klugman, but he had heard of him. He knew that he had worked for the SOE in Bari for over two years. Interestingly enough, Petrovich was fairly certain that he was the intelligence officer for the Yugoslav section. And, he had also heard that Klugman was instrumental in switching British support from Mihailovich to Tito.

If Red was willing to go to such lengths to keep British support with Tito, he had a different goal. And saving O'Donnell and the others was not a part of it.

*   *   *

"SOS . . . SOS . . . One hundred and fifty American crewmembers in need of rescue . . . many sick and wounded . . . advise . . . SOS . . . SOS."

For the last two months, the British had received transmissions indicating downed airmen in Yugoslavia. OSS Agent George Musulin paced. Why was no one taking these seriously?

"It has to be a trap," replied a British Agent.

Musulin, who had spent time in the Mihailovich camp, looked at Vujnovich and shook his head. They were at their wits end with British insistence that Mihailovich was a Nazi collaborator. If anyone knew that was a false accusation, it was Musulin. He had personally witnessed numerous Chetnik attacks against the Nazis. He didn't need any so-called British intelligence to tell him otherwise.

"We cannot jeopardize any of our men. This is obviously

a ploy to lure us into Yugoslavia. At which time, Mihailovich would turn us over to the Nazis," the British agent argued. "I will not authorize any such mission. It would be suicide."

"What if you're wrong?" countered Musulin. "Can you live with abandoning them there for the Nazis to find? Our boys deserve better than that."

"And if I am right? And we send 'our boys' to their demise? Then what?"

"I know Mihailovich. I know him better than any of you. I believe him. Send me in. I'm willing to take that risk."

"Absolutely not. At this point, it is our belief that these transmissions are Nazi generated and we cannot risk sending anyone, not even you, into Yugoslavia. Until there is evidence to the contrary, there will be no such mission." With that, the British agent left the room.

Musulin was pissed. Those were American men stranded in Yugoslavia! They should be going in! The Brits had no right to prevent a rescue mission. What was their problem?

Oh, he knew what their problem was. They were fooled into thinking that the Partisans only wanted to liberate Yugoslavia from the Nazis. But Musulin knew better. He knew what Tito was doing over there. He was sabotaging Allied efforts in Yugoslavia by attacking the Chetniks at every opportunity. The Chetniks were forced to fight Tito nearly as often as they were fighting the Nazis.

Tito was smart, thought Musulin. He had the Soviets helping him with his propaganda. Tito's Partisans took credit for each battle the Chetniks won. Every Chetnik-sabotaged train that blew up, Tito said was Partisan work. Oh yeah, Tito knew what he was doing. And if you asked Musulin, it wasn't to win the war for the Allies. And the worst part was that he didn't care how many of his own people he sacrificed to achieve his goals.

Musulin had personally witnessed how little the Chetniks

had. Their weapons and ammunition levels were dangerously low, their food supply even lower. The peasants had hardly enough to feed their families, yet they did what they could to ensure that the soldiers were fed. They did not have much in the way of military clothing or shoes for that matter. And now they had even less, since the Allies had switched their support from Mihailovic to Tito.

But they did have something more valuable than any of the ammunition and supplies the Allies gave to Tito and his Partisans. They had heart. They were determined to keep their country from falling under Nazi control and they would take all measures necessary to kick them the hell out.

Mihailovic was not setting a trap. Musulin knew that with his entire being. He also knew that Vujnovich was just as sure. Vujnovich's contacts in Washington told him that the Mihailovic camp was sending Washington the names of the Airmen as they were rescued so that their families wouldn't worry.

Musulin didn't get it. Both the Americans and the British wanted to stop Hitler and to free Europe of his claws.

But on days like today, it felt like they were on opposing sides of this mess.

* * *

Mihailovic was certain that the British were intercepting the messages and not communicating them to the Americans. And that pissed him off. So he arranged for a combined group of Serbian and American soldiers to work together. They were desperately trying to develop a code that only the Americans in Italy would understand. Mihailovich tapped his fingers on the table as he thought of them sitting in their tent with piles of crumbled papers scattered on the floor around them- desperation and frustration evident in each tightly formed ball on the ground.

He no longer trusted the British. The Communists had moles everywhere. And he was sure that they had made their way into British intelligence. If he could just get the information directly to the Americans, in a way that only they could understand, he was confident that he could coordinate a rescue. He just had to get the message to them. In his frustration to get the message out and to get a response, he sent his last message in the clear.

"Please advise the American Air Ministry that there are more than one hundred American aviators in our midst . . . We notified the English Supreme Command for the Mediterranean . . . The English replied that they would send an officer to take care of the evacuation.

Meanwhile, to date this has not been done . . . It would be better still if the Americans, and not the British, take part in the evacuation."

Mihailovic knew the last sentence sounded like a rip on the British, but at this point he didn't care. The British had abandoned him and his men. Abandoned his people. He still tried to work with them but they tested his patience day in and day out. He had no other choice than to go directly to the Americans if their men were ever going to see their families again.

The transmission had to be good enough to grab their attention. Something they couldn't ignore.

Shuffling though the paperwork on the table, he shoved his hands through his hair in frustration. He didn't know how much longer her could hide the growing number of downed airmen. As that number increased so did the chances of being discovered by the Nazis. Desperate for a breakthrough, he crossed himself and prayed for God to give him guidance.

*   *   *

At the camp at Pranjane, several American officers were gathered inside one of the village homes. As they strategized about the upcoming sabotage mission with the Chetniks, the door flew open and an American soldier ran in.

"Sirs, they need you at the radio."

In another tent nearby, they found the Americans charged with developing the code, grinning from ear to ear.

"We think we've done it. It'll confuse both the Germans and the British, but our guys should be able to decode it. We think it's our best shot." One of the officers read the intended message aloud. The others scratched their heads and smiled.

At their approval, the airman sat in front of the radio. He said a silent prayer then sent the transmission. Now all they had to do was sit back and hope that the Americans in Italy would decipher it and rescue them. And fast.

CHAPTER 12

"Mudcat Driver to CO, APO 520. 150 Yanks are in Yugo. Shoot us workhorses. Ask British about job. Our challenge first letter of bombardier's name, color of Banana Nose Benignos Scarf."

THE MESSAGE, ALONG with strings of numbers, came through on the all-American link. So an American intelligence officer took on the task of decoding it.

He shut his eyes and tried to clear his thoughts. When he opened them, he ran through the words again, looking for a pattern. It took epic concentration to determine the nature of the words and numbers. He scanned the transmission over and over again, focusing until a pattern emerged.

He jumped at the pounding on the door and lost his train of thought.

"Go away!" he shouted and focused back on the transmission. A few minutes later, the door opened and a fellow US Airman walked into the room.

"Why is it that when I need some peace and quiet to put my damn thoughts together, the entire airbase decides they need to walk in and out of this room!" The intruder winced and quickly retreated from the room.

Frustrated by the constant interruptions, he yanked open the door and looked for his secretary. "Do not interrupt me for any reason. Unless it is an officer that outranks me, tell whoever comes by that I'm busy." He slammed the door and turned the lock.

He sat down at his desk and scratched his head as he dissected the message. Where did he leave off? The pattern he found moments before had faded.

The numbers meant something. He just knew it.

He broke them apart again, putting them into various patterns. Did they represent letters? If they did, he couldn't see it. What were they?

Deciding to step away for a minute, he poured a cup of thick, stale coffee. Hopefully, the caffeine would kick start his brain again. Sipping the hot liquid, he peered out the window. As always, the base was busy with activity. War. Never a day's rest for a soldier.

Soldiers. They were all name, rank, and serial number. *That's it*, he thought. Serial numbers! The numbers *had* to be serial numbers. Putting his theory to test, he bolted back to his desk and grabbed the transmission. He was right.

The serial numbers identified the soldiers. That was a huge breakthrough. But there were still other numbers in between the serial numbers. What did they represent?

"OK. I know *who* you are. Now I just need to figure out the rest. What are you telling us?" he gnawed on his pencil as he ran through different scenarios.

"The serial numbers tell us that you're our guys. I got that. But where are you?" He closed his eyes. His eyes flew open as it dawned on him. "Is that what you're telling me?"

He crossed out the serial numbers. Scanning the remaining

numbers and saw the pattern. They were coordinates. They had
the serial numbers of the soldiers and the latitude and longitude
of their location!

He jumped from the desk and scrambled for the door. It
wouldn't open and he remembered he had locked it earlier. He
struggled with the lock until it finally opened and bolted out of
the room to look for the commander of the 459th Bomb Group,
Major Christi. He found him with Petrovich.

"Sir, the numbers are serial numbers separated by the
coordinates of their location. I'm still working on the rest."

"Good work, officer. Let me take a look at that." Major Christi
took the transmission and read it. His eyes widened as a grin
spread across his face. "Well, I'll be damned. 'Mudcat Driver?
Banana Nose Benigno?' Those are my men!"

* * *

"It's been three days since we sent that last message, and they
still haven't responded. Maybe they couldn't break the code,"
said O'Donnell. He was sitting under a tree with Wallace and
Branko. The afternoon breeze drifted around them, softly
rustling the leaves above.

"Either that or they are still ignoring us," Wallace replied.
He stretched his legs out in front of him and crossed them at
the ankles. He linked his hands behind his head and leaned
back against the tree trunk. "We can only pray that someone
tries to figure it out. Eventually, if for nothing else, out of sheer
curiosity."

O'Donnell sat cross-legged in the field, and chewed on a
blade of grass as he thought about their situation. It was starting
to look like they might never get rescued. And every day they
spent hidden by the Chetniks was riskier than the day before.

It'd been months. Eventually, the Germans would discover
them. The war couldn't go on forever. And if, God forbid, they

lost, what would happen to all of them-including the Serbs who risked everything to help them? He shuddered at the thought.

"Cold?" asked Wallace.

"No, just thinking about this mess, that's all. It looks like we may never get out of here. And if the Germans find us, what will happen to the Serbs for helping us?"

"That's why WE have to win this war. All we can do is keep trying and, in the mean time, do what we can to defeat the Nazis. As for the message, they'll figure it out. Eventually."

Branko laid in the grass with his hands behind his head and quietly whistled a tune as he stared up into the sky. After several minutes, he stood and stretched his hands high above his head. He looked down at O'Donnell and Wallace. "Eat?" he asked.

"Might as well," said O'Donnell. "I know they are working on another sabotage against the Nazis. Let's eat and then see what we can do to help."

They walked back to camp in silence. Uncertainty weighed deeply on them. As soldiers, they were trained to survive. They knew that being shot down in enemy territory was a risk they all took. They also knew they had it much better than any of them could have anticipated. And they were all more than grateful.

But even with the extreme hospitality the Serbian villagers and Chetniks showed them, they still wished for an Allied rescue. They wanted to get back to base and eventually go home. Every day they didn't get discovered by the Germans was a blessing. But how long could their luck hold out?

Branko slapped O'Donnell on the back and put his arm around his shoulder. O'Donnell looked at the young soldier and laughed. "OK, young Chetnik. Let's eat."

*   *   *

The downed American soldiers sat around the radio and wished for a response from their last transmission. It had been a few days and they were losing hope by the hour. The anxious silence in the room was interrupted by the loud voice over the radio.

"Standby for aircraft, 31 July, 2200 hours..."

Chairs flew back across the room as the American officers jumped out of them and scrambled outside to share the good news with the rest of the camp.

"They heard us! They got our message!" they shouted with joy. "They are sending an aircraft!"

A nearby officer whooped loudly, waving his hat in the air. The others laughed and joined in. Some cried tears of joy at the thought of going home. The rest of the soldiers hugged and cheered as the news cascaded. All across camp, men toasted each other with their new favorite drink, Slivovitza.

"Yes!" cheered Wallace. "Our boys are coming to get us, O'Donnell. It's just a matter of time now." He grabbed O'Donnell and hugged him hard.

"It sure is!" he replied, grinning like a child on Christmas morning. He put his arm around Wallace's shoulder and looked around. Everyone was celebrating!

Wallace laughed as he watched the excitement around them. "You'd think the Serbs just won the war! They are about as happy as we are!"

"It's humbling, isn't it? I wonder what would happen if they were in a similar situation in the States?"

"I'd like to think we would do the same for them," Wallace replied.

O'Donnell let go of Wallace and put his hands in his pockets. He watched as the men continued to celebrate. They had a long way yet to go. They still had to get past the Nazis. But even with that threat, this was the best news any of them have heard in a very long time.

Branko walked over and handed O'Donnell and Wallace a small cup each. With a wide smile, he winked at them as he filled each cup with a small amount of Slivovitza.

"You think we can get this stuff back home?" O'Donnell asked Wallace as they drank.

"I sure hope so."

"So," O'Donnell continued after his drink, "the allies know we're here. Now how the heck are they going to get us out?"

CHAPTER 13

O'DONNELL WOKE UP earlier than usual. He'd tossed and turned the entire night as he obsessed about the potential rescue. He stared up at the ceiling, waiting for the early morning rays of dawn to filter through his window. When dawn finally arrived, he dressed and stepped outside. He wasn't the only one who couldn't sleep. Several soldiers, both Serbian and American, were up and about. It seemed that everyone was too excited to worry about lack of sleep.

O'Donnell saw Wallace and Branko drinking coffee at a nearby table and joined them.

"Good morning. I guess you had a hard time sleeping too," O'Donnell said to Wallace as he sat next to him on the wooden bench.

"Too excited, I suppose." Wallace carefully sipped his coffee. "Branko says that General Mihailovic has decided to pay us a visit. He heard the news and wants to be here to help coordinate things. I guess he's supposed to be here later this morning."

"I wonder what he's like," O'Donnell muttered. He could only imagine General Mihailovich. After all, he was the commander of over three hundred thousand troops. O'Donnell pictured him as highly egotistical - barking out orders and demanding the peasants and soldiers to run to his beck and call.

Even worse, this was the man that went from being a highly regarded freedom fighter - revered enough to be on the cover of <u>Time Magazine</u> as the ultimate symbol of freedom - to being classified as a ruthless enemy in the span of just a few years. Which description depicted the real Mihailovic?

O'Donnell thought of the Chetnik soldiers and people that he had encountered from the very first day he was shot down in Yugoslavia. Milka and her brothers, Slavko and Anda, the old woman, Milos, Branko and all of the countless villagers and soldiers along the way.

They were also a part of Mihailovic. For O'Donnell, that was enough to create a curiosity about Mihailovic that was short of obsession. He wanted to meet the man that inspired so much loyalty, and yet so much controversy, all at the same time.

He didn't have to wait long. Mihailovic arrived about an hour later. He walked into Pranjane, his sack on his back and surrounded by dozens of laughing children who blatantly adored him. He patted one of the children on the head as the child spoke to him with a lot of enthusiasm. He smiled at the child as he replied to him. The child grinned from ear to ear and saluted the General.

Mihailovic was average height and had a wiry build. His blue eyes twinkled from behind his horn-rimmed glasses as he spoke to the children. They laughed at whatever he said and continued to follow him into camp. He scratched his salt and pepper beard as he spoke to them. His military stature was evident in the officer's uniform he wore. Ironically, there was a certain underlying strength that seemed to emanate from him that was not diminished by the humble demeanor he displayed towards the children and the peasants that gathered around him.

The crowd of peasants continued to grow. He waved one of his soldiers over and spoke quietly to him. The soldier chuckled and nodded in response. General Mihailovic smiled at his soldier and shook his hand. The soldier walked away, beaming from the General's words.

"He isn't what I expected, that's for sure," observed O'Donnell.

"What did you expect? Horns and a tail?" Wallace laughed in response.

"Not really sure, to be honest. I guess I thought he'd at least be driven in by some of his men. And I figured he'd be a lot more, I don't know, rigid."

"I've heard that he believes respect is earned, not demanded or forced," Wallace replied. "And from what I've gathered while I've been here is that he has definitely earned their respect."

His interpreter introduced Mihailovic to the American airmen. After introductions, they all proceeded to the nearby field where the Chetniks entertained the General and Americans with songs and dance.

"Chicha Drazha!" men called out to Mihailovic as they greeted him or asked him a question.

"What does that mean?" asked O'Donnell.

"Uncle Drazha. It's what the people and his men call him."

Afterwards, the American airmen gathered with General Mihailovic nearby. He sat on a rock and looked out at the unshaved American soldiers that surrounded him. The General shifted his gaze towards the heavens as he gathered his thoughts.

With the help of his interpreter, he told the Americans, "I admire Americans and the freedom loving principles and ideals that America offers. I hope that one day ALL of the people of Yugoslavia will one day again enjoy all those very same freedoms.

"I am disappointed that the Allies have forsaken us. I am fairly sure that the British are the ones who have pushed for the mistaken support of Tito. I am also well aware of the false reports that Tito has been broadcasting about my men and me. It makes me furious to hear those lies. But I am not surprised."

He paused for a moment then looked at each of the airmen, holding their gazes for emphasis, "I know my people and as such, I know they have taken care of each of you. That is our way. When you go back to America, please tell everyone the truth about the Chetniks and our homeland. Do not allow Tito's and Stalin's lies to prevail.

"How strange," he continued with watery eyes, "the bitter ironies of war. I am slaughtering thousands of German troops, fighting for the freedom of my people while Tito has befriended the Nazis for his own gain. He deceives the Allies with the help of Stalin. And as such, he is now the favored one in Yugoslavia and I have somehow become the enemy.

"However, I have not lost all hope. We will continue to resist the Nazis as we have done throughout this war. We have no choice if we are to survive as a people and as a nation." He paused as he took off his round wire-rimmed glasses and rubbed his eyes. He replaced the eyeglasses and continued. "And it is my hope that the Allied nations will see the error they have made, and that they will return their support to us."

O'Donnell was speechless. *This man is still loyal to us?*

Mihailovic admitted that he had made mistakes and that he had some regrets. However, every decision, every act was made with the intention of ridding his country of the Nazis and their Axis partners and to ensure that Yugoslavia would remain a free country.

"As for the evacuation, we will turn the field, that we used earlier for entertainment, into an airstrip. I will have over eight thousand of my men surrounding it within twenty-four hours. If the Nazis somehow discover the evacuation, my men can hold them off until you are evacuated.

"As for logistics. There are approximately six thousand Nazi

troops stationed about twelve miles away at the city of Cacak."
At this, many of the airmen groaned.

"Don't be concerned," assured General Mihailovic. "The Nazis may be far better armed, but they would have trouble maneuvering the difficult mountainous terrain in their vehicles. And to resort to hill fighting would be to their disadvantage." He paused as he looked out at his Chetniks. And then with pride he added, "Because when it comes to fighting in the these mountains and hills, my men are by far the best."

"Woohoo! Yea!" cheered the men.

"We get started in the morning," concluded Mihailovic.

Everyone dispersed. The General stood and greeted the airmen individually. Many asked him to sign different pieces of memorabilia. Some offered their thoughts on the current situation, others their apologies and all offered their assurances that they would go back and tell the truth about him and his Chetniks.

The General invited O'Donnell and several others to join him for dinner at a nearby farmhouse. The family who lived there welcomed them all in and seated them while they brought out food and placed it on the table in front of them. To celebrate, their son grabbed his accordion and began playing festive Serbian songs.

Everyone was singing and dancing and toasting to victory.

"Zivio!" toasted the owner of the farmhouse as he clinked his glass with O'Donnell's.

O'Donnell laughed as a few of the Americans attempted to dance the traditional Serbian dance known as kolo. They held hands with the locals and tried to follow the complicated steps of the dance. As the Americans hopped their way among the peasants, General Mihailovic leaned towards O'Donnell.

"Tell me about your family," he said through his interpreter. O'Donnell told him about his mother, father, brother and sister.

"I have a fellow airman who I consider to be my brother," O'Donnell continued. "His name is Petrovich."

"Petrovich? How ironic that your friend is a Serb! That is something we can toast to." The General laughed as he lifted his glass.

"He is ethnically Serbian, but a true blue American soldier. I think you'd be proud to know him."

"Maybe one day I will have the honor. Now tell me, what are your plans when this war is over?" he asked with sincere interest.

After an evening of singing, dancing, and toasting to victory, O'Donnell collapsed onto his bed and replayed the events of the evening in his head. General Mihailovic had spent most of the evening engaged in conversation with the Airmen.

He also shared pieces of himself that O'Donnell found intriguing. Although Mihailovic was confident in his actions and decisions, he still had regrets as to how he had handled various situations. He reiterated his deep hurt that the Allies viewed him as an enemy – and his astonishment that they viewed Tito as their only ally in Yugoslavia.

O'Donnell also saw the anger in his eyes when he spoke about the Partisans. There was definitely no love there. Interestingly, Mihailovic mentioned that if the Partisans and the Chetniks had joined forces to fight the Nazis, their combined strength would have liberated Yugoslavia from the Nazis. However, instead of working together to win the war, Tito and his Partisans were attacking the Chetniks at every opportunity.

O'Donnell remembered Wallace had shared a story that confirmed the General's claim. On one particular mission Wallace and some of the other airmen and the Chetniks were engaged in a battle against the Germans. They were deep in the midst of fighting when the Partisans attacked the Chetniks from behind. They had to fight the Nazis on one end and the Partisans on the other. They barely made it out alive. The Partisans essentially helped the Germans in their battle against the Chetniks. The General also discussed the horrible situation with the Ustasha. He told O'Donnell of the countless concentration camps the Croatian Ustasha had and the gruesome murders being committed against hundreds of thousands of helpless Serbs, Jews and Gypsies. He admitted that fighting three fronts - against the Nazis, the Ustasha and the Partisans - was becoming more and more difficult. But he would not give up.

Before he succumbed to sleep, O'Donnell thought about the many sides of a man who was gravely misunderstood. O'Donnell swore that when he got back to base, he would set the record straight and get the Chetniks the support they deserved.

CHAPTER 14

"TITO WON'T LIKE it," argued a British SOE agent.

"It will cause irreparable damage to our alliance with Tito. It could have disastrous repercussions," Red agreed.

"This isn't about Tito. It's about going in and evacuating our men from Yugoslavia," Petrovich countered. "If the tables were turned and Tito had to make this very same decision, would he leave his Partisans to be sitting ducks for the Nazis? Tito liking it or not liking it is irrelevant."

"It is very relevant. It's called an alliance, which requires trust. If we break his trust, that will cause a rift in our alliance. That could affect our strategy in Yugoslavia."

"Red, if Tito is such a good ally, he will understand our need to evacuate our men. In fact, he should be supportive of that. Unless, of course, he's scared that we might find out that Mihailovich isn't really collaborating with the Nazis. And that would mean that the information we have been getting from Tito and his Partisans has been false."

"Always the devil's advocate, Petrovich. Our intelligence has confirmed the reports coming from the Partisans. It's the principle of the matter."

Petrovich shook his head in disgust. He didn't put much

credibility in British intelligence when it came to Yugoslavia. Over the past few months he had learned enough about the situation there to know better. There were too many factors playing out on that battlefield.

Communism was just as much of a threat as the Nazis, as far as he was concerned. And even though he couldn't prove it, yet, he had a strong feeling that establishing a communist Yugoslavia was the ultimate agenda for Tito and Stalin. Defeating the Germans was a means to an end for Tito.

After overhearing Red and the others, he knew that Tito's agenda was something that some of the SOE and even some of his own OSS were favoring. He worried that the Communists would stoop to any level to achieve their goals. And he wouldn't put it past them to falsify reports to get the support they need.

"I don't think it's the principle of trust," shouted Petrovich. "I think it's a matter of life and death for our American soldiers. There is nothing more important than that. Musulin and Vujnovich feel the same way.

"With all due respect, those are Americans over there. That should, in itself, make this an American decision."

"This base is under British command," retorted Red. "If the decision is made to evacuate, then the British should perform that operation."

Petrovich knew that Red was right; the base was under British command. But his gut told him that the British were being misled about what was really going on in Yugoslavia. The communist moles within the British SOE made sure that Churchill supported Tito, but did Churchill understand the ramifications? Petrovich did not think for a minute that Churchill supported a potential communist Yugoslavia. How deep was the deception within his ranks? If his gut was right, that would mean that a British led operation to evacuate would not end well.

Petrovich thought of O'Donnell. He didn't know for certain that he was trapped in Yugoslavia. But there was a chance. And for O'Donnell's sake, Petrovich hoped that the Americans would take the lead.

*   *   *

Musulin would not back down.

"If there is to be any mission, then we will take the lead," proclaimed the British officer discussing the transmission with Musulin, an American OSS Agent.

"No way. Those are our men. We should take the lead," argued Musulin.

"I must insist. This base is under British control. Please remember that we are on the same side of this war. You should feel confident that we would treat this as if we were going in after our own British airmen."

"We are on the same side. So there should be no reason you or any of our British friends should prohibit us from going in after our own," Musulin countered.

He was determined that the mission would be approved and that Americans would take the lead. He reasoned. He argued. But the British objections were so strong, that the Americans sent their appeal all the way to President Roosevelt.

Days later, a deeply frustrated Musulin sat at his desk, his hands fisted in his hair as he formulated yet another argument in favor of him going in to the Mihailovic camp. Argument after argument filtered through his thoughts and all made perfect sense to him. So why didn't it make any sense to the British officers that made the decisions?

Vujnovich found him at his desk and nodded in

understanding. But this time, he came to Musulin with a different message.

"Keep pulling at your hair like that, you won't have any by the time you get back to the States."

"Funny guy," retorted Musulin. "I'm losing my mind with this one. Just trying to find a different angle to get someone to see our point of view with this."

"Well, stop losing your mind. President Roosevelt came through for us. He personally approved a rescue mission," Vujnovich said as he watched Musulin slowly rise from his chair in disbelief.

"That's right. Get your gear together. Stop looking for an argument to get you in. Start planning your mission. You're going in."

* * *

Petrovich was hungry. But he was too mad to eat. How could anyone be so damn stubborn? Why wouldn't the British budge? He looked down at his food and his stomach churned.

The door opened and General MacKenzie walked through. Petrovich watched as the General scanned the room. His eyes found Petrovich and he stalked to him. Petrovich rose.

"General," he said as he saluted.

"Petrovich. I know this has been a personal mission for you since O'Donnell's been missing. That's why I came to find you as soon as I heard."

Petrovich's stomach fell as he considered the General's words. Only bad news could make him come looking for Petrovich.

"Sir. What have you heard?"

"We are sending in an Air Crew Rescue Unit to assess the situation, code naming the mission as Halyard. If O'Donnell is there, we will know soon enough."

Petrovich let out the breath he didn't know he was holding

and rubbed his eyes. "That's great news, General. Who's commanding the mission?" asked Petrovich.

"Musulin," answered the General.

"Thank God!" exclaimed Petrovich as a relieved grin spread across his face.

Later that day, Petrovich learned from Musulin that two other Americans, OSS Master Sargent Michael Rajacich and radio operator Arthur Jibilian, were going to join him on his mission. Petrovich was a little concerned about Jibilian, as he had heard that he had been in Yugoslavia before, but with the Partisans. But Jibilian was an American first and foremost. He had to trust that.

"We've been ordered not to give any political commitment on behalf of any of the Allies. This is a rescue mission only. Nothing more. And the Chetniks are not to get the wrong impression," explained Musulin to Petrovich.

Musulin had spent time on OSS missions in Yugoslavia with the Mihailovic camp. He had gotten to know Mihailovic and his men very well over the course of his time there. He didn't believe the propaganda that was being perpetrated against Mihailovic. However irritated he might be about that, his foremost concern with this mission was for a safe return of the American airmen.

"Vujnovich has been working on trying to come up with a plan to get us there safely. First, we will verify the transmission and see if there are truly airmen in need of evacuation. If they are there, and I am confident that they are, then we will formulate a plan to get them out of there." Musulin put his hand on Petrovich's shoulder and added, "If O'Donnell's there, we will bring him home."

Later that afternoon, Petrovich sat on his bed and thought about the upcoming mission. They were scheduled to go out late that night. He rested his face in his hands as he thought about O'Donnell.

It had been months since he was shot down over Yugoslavia. And although they hadn't heard anything from him, Petrovich knew he was alive. He couldn't explain it, but deep down in his soul, he felt that O'Donnell was alive and with the Chetniks.

*   *   *

July 31, 1944

Musulin, Rajacich and Jibilian were ready. The C-47, painted black so that the dark night would camouflage it from the Nazis, waited on the tarmac, ready to embark on their mission.

They were about to fly through enemy skies and jump into unknown territory. No one ever really knew what would be waiting for them once they were on the ground, despite the best-laid plans. And any mission conducted in the dark added another level of complications and danger. Regardless, Musulin was anxious to get the mission started and complete it successfully.

After takeoff, they sat quietly in the plane. The cabin cooled substantially as they increased their elevation. Minor turbulence shook the plane, but overall the ascent was smooth. Musulin rubbed his hands on his legs and silently thanked God for the smooth flight.

As they neared the drop zone in Pranjane, his heart raced and adrenaline pulsed through him. He would have been happier with an all American crew, but the circumstances of being under British command warranted a joint mission. So, the pilot and jumpmaster were both British. But, with all the British opposition to the evacuation, Musulin was happy to be on this mission at all.

He and the other two airmen stood and checked their parachutes and other gear, preparing for their jump. Satisfied that everything was in order, they waited for the jump light to turn green.

Several minutes later they were still waiting. Musulin yelled out to the jumpmaster, "What's going on? Why haven't we been given the signal?"

"There aren't any ground signals over the drop zone," shouted the jumpmaster. "And they haven't responded to our signals."

Musulin couldn't understand it. Why wouldn't Mihailovich's men respond? They knew they were coming. Something didn't add up.

"It's too dangerous. Without the ground signals, we can't complete the mission. We have to abort," shouted the jumpmaster.

At the command the pilot turned the plane around and returned to Italy. Musulin returned to his seat. Confused, he contemplated what went wrong.

Missions were aborted often. If everything was not aligned correctly, it was better to abort than to take unnecessary risks. Musulin was disappointed, but he didn't want to jump into the hands of the Nazis. So they had no choice but to accept it and focus on trying the mission again tomorrow.

The next night, they once again boarded the C-47. Unlike the previous night, Musulin cursed the unlucky weather. Flying over the mountains of Yugoslavia, the plane violently bounced up and down and left and right in the highly turbulent air. In the night sky, flashing lightning eerily illuminated the interior of the plane. The crack of thunder boomed throughout the plane, jolting the men from their deep thoughts. The storm raged around them as the plane tried to fight its way through the turbulence then dropped several feet. In the interest of safety, both during the flight and after they jumped; the mission was aborted, again.

Back at base, Petrovich watched the planes land. He kicked the tarmac, dumbstruck that this second mission had aborted too! He hoped that Musulin's next mission would finally get them into Yugoslavia. It had to.

The third night, the plane took off into the night. Musulin and the others sat in the plane, with their gear on, anxiously waiting for a successful drop. As they approached Yugoslavia, Musulin became more hopeful.

"This looks like the night. I guess it's true," Musulin said, "third time's the cha . . . ." The plane jolted strongly to the right as enemy anti-aircraft fire exploded around them. The night sky lit around them as bombs and missiles exploded all around the plane.

Musulin and the others held on tightly as the plane zigzagged through the air to avoid the bombs that exploded around them. His disappointment mounted as he realized that with this kind of antiaircraft fire, the chances of a successful mission dropped with each violent jerk of the plane.

"The flak is too intense!" shouted the pilot, a British flier, confirming Musulin's thoughts. "It's too dangerous! We need to turn back!" With that, he maneuvered the plane through the massive flak surrounding the plane and flew back to base. Once again, Musulin, Jibilian and Rajacich were disappointed and cursed their luck.

*   *   *

"A series of unfortunate events," commented Red after Musulin and his crew returned the third time. "Perhaps it just isn't meant to be."

"You'd like that, wouldn't you?" Petrovich growled. "But, we won't give up."

"As if I have any control over things like weather and flak. Petrovich, I've said it before, you have become quite the conspiracy theorist!"

"A realist, Red. I just call it like I see it."

*   *   *

Musulin, Jibilian and Rajacich prepared for the fourth try. They were more anxious this time than any of the last three. This had to be the last attempt. There couldn't possibly be anything to stop them this time.

They were suspicious of the British who joined them on their missions. Musulin was especially weary of their motives. Last night, as he replayed the events of the past few nights, he'd learned that on their first attempt, the pilot had flown to the wrong coordinates! When he reviewed the specifics of the first night's flight, he noticed that the drop coordinates that were given to the pilot were not the same ones originally outlined within the mission. That was the reason they didn't have any ground signals; they weren't in the right area. That would have been a rookie mistake, and the pilot that night was no rookie.

He couldn't prove that the other two were deliberate attempts to sabotage the mission by flying directly into a storm or into an area with known fighting. But he had his suspicions.

Regardless, this was their latest attempt, and Musulin was confident that this time it would happen. It had to. What were the chances something would go wrong again? However, since he knew that the pilot flew to the wrong area the first night, he decided to double check their drop point soon after takeoff.

"Verify the coordinates of our drop zone," demanded Musulin.

The pilot complied and read off the coordinates. Musulin checked the map to verify they were flying to the right destination. They were planning on sending them straight into Partisan territory! He threw the map at the pilot.

"Are you crazy?" he exploded. "Where did you get this?"

"Just following orders," he replied.

Angrier than before, he turned to head back into the cargo when he noticed a young solider with a red star on his cap sitting in the back of the plane. The red star was indicative of the Partisans.

"What the hell is he doing here?" screamed out Musulin. "A Partisan on our plane during my mission?"

"He's our jump master."

"That commie is supposed to push me and my crew out of this plane? I'm supposed to trust him to send me to the right place? Into his enemy's hands? Are you guys trying to get us killed?"

The pilot swallowed hard and his eyes widened in fear of Musulin's reaction. Musulin was already a very large intimidating man. He was even more intimidating as his voice boomed throughout the noisy plane. The Partisan scooted as far back as he could and looked away.

"You can forget this mission. I am aborting it. Take us back . . . Now!"

"You don't have the authority to abort the mission."

"I couldn't care less what authority I have or don't have. My men and I are not jumping out of this plane. I said ABORT!"

As the plane turned around and headed back to Italy, Musulin was speechless. What was going on? Could the British really be sabotaging this mission? They were allies! Would they purposely endanger the lives of Musulin and his crew?

Whatever was going on, he wanted to believe that it was purely coincidental.

Back at base, Musulin and the others discussed the series of aborted missions. They all agreed that it couldn't happen again. If it did, it couldn't be called a series of coincidences any more. But they were still worried about the rumors of the communist moles within the British SOE.

"Do you think the moles are that far into the SOE that they could be purposely sabotaging our attempts to get into Mihailovich's camp?" asked Jibilian.

"I don't know," replied Musulin. "The problem is that at this point, those are just rumors. The British are our allies, I don't want to think they would sabotage efforts to retrieve our men from behind enemy lines."

"Well, the British officials in London wouldn't. But who is to say that those down the ranks aren't being fooled by these supposed moles?" countered Rajacich.

"We don't really know anything for sure right now. So all we can do is hope that we are wrong about the moles. Tomorrow night we try again. The chances of us not succeeding again are slim to none."

The next night, they tried for the fifth time to be dropped into Mihailovic territory. Once again, their anticipation was high. They checked their gear and verified the coordinates. All looked good.

The light turned green and they prepared to jump. Musulin braced himself on the doorway and looked into the jump area. He couldn't see much through the dark. Rechecking his gear one more time, something caught his eye below.

At first he wasn't quite sure what it was, but it made him uneasy. He took a better look. Flashes of light pierced the night sky below as a battle raged directly beneath them. Right where they were going to jump!

He shoved himself back away from the doorway, knocking over the other men.

"What are you doing?" shouted the jumpmaster.

"You are sending us straight into a battle! Either you guys are purposely trying to sabotage this mission or you don't know what the hell you are doing. Either way, this mission is aborted . . . again!" shouted Musulin.

Musulin stormed across base straight into Vujnovich's office. He slammed his hands on his desk and leaned forward.

"If this mission is ever going to happen, it will be without a dust of British influence. I don't know what is going on with them, but I've had enough."

Frustrated and fuming, he replayed the events of the evening. Vujnovich listened intently and swore under his breath as he took it all in.

"I want an American plane. I want an American crew. And I mean ALL American . . . no one else on that plane," demanded Musulin.

Vujnovich stood up and stuck out his hand. Musulin took it and shook.

"All American it is," agreed Vujnovich.

CHAPTER 15

July 31, 1944

As promised, General Mihailovich's men surrounded Pranjane. They were prepared to keep the Germans at bay if it became necessary. Their orders were simple and direct.

The task was daunting as airmen were scattered in a hundred mile radius around Pranjane. Regardless, both the Serbs and the airmen were committed to ensuring a successful evacuation.

O'Donnell looked at the makeshift airstrip. Before today it was a narrow plateau that was used for grazing cattle and sheep. He shook his head as he evaluated the parameters of the plateau. It was only one hundred feet wide and about nineteen hundred feet long. Nowhere near enough room for a plane to land or the size of an actual landing strip.

As if the situation wasn't dangerous enough, with the Nazis surrounding them and occasionally flying overhead, now they had to worry if a plane could actually land here.

The men were determined to make it happen. And what a sight to see! O'Donnell grinned as he and hundreds of other Chetniks, airmen and Serbian peasants worked the plateau to create the temporary airstrip. Every available man, woman and child was shoveling, raking, and grading the land to level it as much as possible for a plane to land.

Some of the peasants began singing a song in their native Serbian tongue. Soon all the Chetniks joined in. O'Donnell had no idea what they were singing, but he liked it nonetheless.

"What are they are singing about?" O'Donnell asked.

"Freedom," answered Branko with pride.

Freedom, thought O'Donnell. That's all these people have ever wanted. After all that they had done for him and the other American airmen, he made a silent pledge. If he got out of here safely, he would do what he could to give it to them.

The drop time was scheduled for 2200 hours. At precisely ten o'clock, one hundred and sixty airmen waited breathlessly. It was pitch black outside. It was so dark that many wondered how this would happen without any navigational radio. Others prayed silently for success.

They had no idea the intentions of the Fifteenth Air Force. Some thought that they would be dropping off supplies while others thought they were about to be rescued. All they could do at this point was wait and see what would happen.

Several minutes passed. With each passing minute, they slowly lost hope. But at 10:38PM, they heard a faint drone of a plane in the distance.

"Are they late?" whispered O'Donnell.

"Maybe, or it could be a Nazi aircraft searching the area," replied Wallace.

"You think?"

"I don't know. I can't believe they would be this late. Even under these conditions."

"Should we light the flare pots for them?" O'Donnell asked, referring to the three flare pots on either side of the airstrip that would identify the width of the strip.

"Might be too dangerous. What if it's the Nazis? Then we ruin everything."

Not being able to identify the aircraft, they decided not to light the flares. They hid in the bushes surrounding the makeshift airstrip as the plane flew overhead. After it had passed, they all walked away. Their hopes of rescue plummeted.

The next day they tried contacting the headquarters. Once again, they were unable to establish communication. All they could do was gather at the airstrip again that evening and hope that the Fifteenth Air force would come.

Sitting in the dark, they hoped for a miracle and held their breath as ten o'clock neared. O'Donnell said a silent prayer as he crouched near a tree. They had to come tonight, he thought. They just had to.

As ten o'clock came and went, the reality sank in. No rescue tonight.

August 5, 1944

Hope lowest that it's been in days, O'Donnell and Wallace sat in the warm afternoon sunlight and discussed the events of the past days.

"If they don't come tonight," said O'Donnell "then I think we need to find another way out of here."

"How else can we get out without an air evacuation?" asked Wallace.

"The Chetniks know every nook and cranny in these mountains. I think our only option is to see if we can walk out of here."

"Our chances of survival are greatly diminished if we have to resort to that. There would be too many chances of running into the Nazis." Wallace paused as he drank from his flask.

"True, but we are sitting ducks here, just waiting for them to find us. And if they do, they would slaughter the peasants for hiding us," replied O'Donnell.

"What about the Partisans? The Chetniks are forced to fight the Partisans as often as they have to battle the Nazis. If we run into them, what happens then?"

"I wonder if anyone really knows how messed up it really is here," commented O'Donnell.

That evening, everyone gathered, yet again, at the airstrip. Although they thought it was a long shot, they had no choice but to hope. As ten o'clock drew nearer, they held their breath and waited.

The night was dark with minimal moonlight to brighten the night. Silence filled the air as they waited. No aircraft in sight and time quickly slipping away, dread filled the men. This was their last hope. They decided to wait a few more minutes, just in case. After fifteen minutes, all hope was gone.

Disappointed, O'Donnell stood to leave the airstrip. But as he was about to leave, he heard a soft noise in the distance. Straining to hear, he cupped his ear and held his breath. As the noise became louder, O'Donnell quickly recognized it. A plane!

Excitement and anticipation filled the air as realization hit that a plane was approaching.

"Should we risk it?" asked O'Donnell. "Should we light the flares?"

Wallace stared at the sky then looked at the hundreds of airmen surrounding the field. "May as well risk it all. Light the flares!"

The night glowed from the flares on both sides of the airstrip. They knew that they were taking a major risk by lighting the flares without confirming the identity of the plane. But at this point, they didn't care.

"We should signal the plane, if it is our guys. They need to know they are in the right spot."

Wallace agreed and signaled the plane with three red flashes.

The plane turned towards them as it spotted the lights. The tension was thick as they waited to identify the plane. The plane descended slowly. With each second, they wondered if they did the right thing.

"Oh my God," said Wallace. "If that is a Nazi plane, we just handed them our location and we are as good as dead."

O'Donnell's heart raced. The plane seemed to be flying in slow motion as he watched its descent. The lives of these men would be determined in the next several minutes. This was it.

"I can't tell if that plane is ours. It's so damn dark and these flares make it so hard to see," O'Donnell replied. "Please God, let it be ours. Please!"

As the plane came in lower, O'Donnell and the others looked for the slightest indication that these were the good guys. Straining to see through the glow of the flares, O'Donnell searched desperately for a sign.

Then he saw it. A white star adorned the fuselage. That was the insignia of the Unites States Army Air Corp!

"It's them!" shouted O'Donnell. "It's our guys! They've found us!"

The field erupted in cheers as the airmen and Chetniks celebrated. The risk had paid off! They watched as the plane passed over them and disappear into the night sky beyond the plateau. And then several minutes later, after it turned around, it flew over them again, and headed back towards Italy.

"What the heck?" wondered O'Donnell. "Where are they going?"

"Maybe they were verifying location first and then plan on getting in touch with us for further instructions," replied Wallace.

Better than nothing, thought O'Donnell. But he couldn't

help being disappointed that they had to wait even longer to know what the plan was going to be.

"Well, at least they saw us. Now they have to come back and get us. We should probably head back and clear this place out." They walked towards the flaring pots to distinguish them when they heard the cheers of the soldiers behind them.

A group of Chetniks ran towards the field carrying packages dropped by the plane. Opening the crates, they found medical supplies and clothing. Excitement was overflowing as the hope of rescue mounted.

"Well, they definitely know we are here. Hopefully this means they'll contact us tomorrow and we can work out some sort of plan to evacuate," Wallace said to O'Donnell.

"At least they dropped off some supplies for the time being. That's something for now. And they'll believe Mihailovich going forward, don't you think?" O'Donnell said as he looked through one of the packages and examined the supplies.

"I'm not sure. But at least they've confirmed our location. It's just a matter of time, now."

Musulin, Rajacich and Jibilian jumped out of the low flying plane. At only eight hundred feet above ground, their parachutes opened immediately and they only had about thirty-seconds before hitting the ground.

Musulin fell the fastest and the hardest as he crashed into a chicken coup.

Feathers and pieces of wood soared through the air. The few chickens that survived balked in a flurry around him as he got to his feet. He looked around and laughed. Of all the places he could land, he would land on top of a bunch of chickens.

Brushing off the dust and debris, he disengaged his parachute and began to look for the other members of his team. He heard Rajacich in the distance and followed his voice.

Musulin found Rajacich hanging from his parachute in a tree.

"You all right?" asked Musulin.

"Yea, I'm OK. Just help me get down from here." Musulin climbed up the tree and cut him down. They had to work quickly. If the Germans spotted them, they only had minutes.

"Let's find Jibilian."

They found him in a nearby cornfield. Fortunately for him, the cornstalks softened his landing.

"Gather our gear. We need to find our soldiers as quickly as possible."

They worked quickly and started walking in the direction of the flares. A peasant woman spotted them and ran as fast as she could until she stood in front of them. Talking fast, she jumped up and down and showered them with hugs and kisses.

"She thinks we are here to liberate them," Musulin explained to his team.

Since he knew the language, Musulin told her that they were not there to free her people, but that they were looking for the Americans that the Chetniks were protecting. Undeterred by his admission, she hugged him again and directed him towards the Mihailovich camp.

"I'm sorry about the chicken coup. Here is a little bit of money to help you repair it," he told her in Serbian. She gratefully accepted the money then hugged and kissed them again, thanking them for helping to free her people.

They were confident now that they were in Chetnik territory. But they still had to find camp and avoid the Germans. They walked in the direction the peasant woman had provided, hoping to come across a friendly Chetnik.

A group of large bearded men drew near the team. They searched around the area obviously looking for something.

From the royal insignia they wore on their hats, Musulin knew they were the Chetniks.

"Musulin!" cried out one of the men as they recognized him from his previous mission among the Chetniks.

"George the American!" said another as he hugged Musulin.

"He's like a movie star!" laughed Rajacich referring to the way the Chetniks greeted Musulin.

But within moments, Rajacich and Jibilian found themselves being bear hugged by the intimidating Chetniks as well.

"Just like movie stars," joked Musulin to Rajacich and Jibilian.

The bearded Chetniks overwhelmed the men with their gratitude. But Musulin knew he had to explain the situation to them before they got the wrong impression. He quickly told them that they were only there to help facilitate a rescue of the American airmen. Not for any other reason. He wanted them to understand that things hadn't changed from the viewpoint of the Allies.

"The support of the Allies is still with Tito," he said.

They said they understood. But by the hopeful looks on their faces, Musulin was sure that they didn't.

The Americans followed the Chetniks towards camp. As they passed a group of trees and entered camp, excitement erupted. Several of the Chetniks recognized Musulin and ran towards him in greeting.

Musulin approached O'Donnell. "I'm Lieutenant George Musulin with the OSS. Our team's official designation is Air Corps Rescue Unit Team Number One."

"Very glad to meet you, I'm Bill O'Donnell of the Fifteenth Air Force," he said as he shook his hand. "Welcome to Pranjane." He laughed, "Am I happy to see you!"

Musulin took in the sight and was amazed at what he saw. He was told to expect about one hundred to a hundred and fifty men. But this looked like much more than that.

"I see you've found the supplies and radios we just dropped. We also have a plan for evacuation." He paused as he absorbed the numbers of men milling around. "We thought we'd find about one hundred and fifty men. This looks like quite a bit more."

"More like two-hundred and fifty. And there are hundreds more in the surrounding areas. And the numbers keep rising," answered O'Donnell.

Two hundred and fifty men and hundreds *in the surrounding areas?* Musulin swallowed hard as he took in the information. This was going to be harder than they thought.

CHAPTER 16

THE NEXT MORNING, Musulin, Rajacich and Jibilian immediately got to work. Time was of the essence and the sooner they put plans into action, the more likely they could avoid detection and capture by the Germans.

The peasants insisted on feeding them as soon as they woke up. They took whatever they had and put together a breakfast for Musulin, Rajacich and Jibilian. The women fussed over the men as the children giggled excitedly. The men laughed and joked as they watched the three Americans eat their breakfast.

"They act like we just conquered the entire German army!" said Jibilian.

"Despite being told otherwise, they think us being here is a sign that Allied support is switching back to Mihailovich. That's the first sign of hope they've had in a long time," answered Musulin.

"Makes me feel guilty accepting their kindness and food. It doesn't look like they have much," added Rajacich.

"No, they don't have much at all. This war has been hell on them." Musulin glanced at peasants that had gathered around to see them. "They barely have enough to eat, not nearly enough resources left to survive, and yet they somehow keep fighting. They just keep going."

"It's humbling," whispered Jibilian.

"It sure is. But they really have no other choice. And it's been like this for generations. It's just their way. I don't know how they sometimes don't say that they've had enough and give in to the invaders," questioned Musulin.

They sat in silence for a few minutes and looked around them as they ate their breakfast and drank their Turkish coffee.

When they had assessed the feasibility of the airstrip for an evacuation, they discovered that it was not long enough to provide a safe landing area for the C-47s, especially if wind conditions worsened. So Musulin and Mihailovic decided that they needed to add an additional seventy-five yards to the length.

Approximately three hundred peasants, including men, women and children, immediately worked on extending the field. They dug, hauled and unloaded dirt, grass and gravel. And when the Americans offered to pay them, they refused.

Jibilian smiled as he watched them hard at work. He was humbled at the kindness and determination these people were showing to help evacuate the Americans. All the while knowing that they would be left behind to continue to fight the Germans on their own.

"You know, I was in the Tito camp for awhile," he said quietly to Musulin.

"I know," replied Musulin.

"I can honestly say that at the time, I had no idea, really, what a Chetnik was. I was told that they were Nazi collaborators and that they were monsters that committed the worst kind of atrocities.

"But in this short amount of time that we've been here, I can honestly say that I haven't seen anything of the sort."

"Between us, Tito has his own agenda. He needs full Allied support, especially if I am right and he plans on taking over

Yugoslavia if this war ever ends." Musulin replied. "And I'd bet that he doesn't plan on reinstating the monarchy."

"We wouldn't let him set up a communist government. He'll be sorely disappointed when this war is over," Rajacich added sipping his coffee.

"I wouldn't be so sure," answered Musulin. "Stalin is backing him. And although I can't prove it, there's some shady stuff going on within the Allies too. There are some Tito sympathizers within our ranks. I sometimes wonder if they are for Tito as an ally against the Germans or for communism in general. I guess we will have to wait and see. The truth has a way of coming out on its own."

O'Donnell joined them as they finished their breakfast. He was curious to hear what the next steps were going to be.

"Good morning," he said as they stood up.

"Good morning," they replied.

"I'm wondering what the next step is. And I'd like to offer up my services if you need any assistance in getting things going."

"I'd say our first course of action is to get this airfield ready for the C-47s to land. So if you've got the inclination, helping them on the field would be a good start.

"We are going to contact headquarters with a status update and then we will get together with Mihailovich and some of the airmen to formulate a final plan. You can join us when we do," Musulin replied.

"I plan on it, Lieutenant. You can count on me."

Jibilian contacted headquarters first. When headquarters confirmed the code, Jibilian and Musulin reported their findings

"There are approximately twenty-six sick or wounded soldiers that need immediate medical attention. Rajacich is currently providing medical supplies to the doctor who is treating the soldiers and peasants.

"However, there are substantially more downed airmen

than we initially anticipated. We originally assumed close to one hundred and fifty. But after a thorough assessment of the situation, we are finding that that number will be closer to two hundred and fifty. And quite possibly much more than that in outlying villages," Musulin reported. They continued with their report until they were satisfied that headquarters had a thorough understanding of the dire situation at hand.

They knew that there was a lot of opposition to their mission. The moles that had found their way into the SOE were determined to continue to mislead the British about Mihailovich. They were not about to let the three OSS agents ruin their plans. So Jibilian, Rajacich and Musulin reported, in great detail, what they could to ensure the support of the Americans in Bari.

Later that day, Musulin, Jibilian and Rajacich held a meeting with a committee consisting of several airmen, Mihailovich and his representatives to formulate a plan of evacuation. They needed to evacuate the men without alerting the Germans that surrounded the area.

Mihailovic listened as the Americans planned. After some thought, through his interpreter, he added, "My men have been instructed to guard Pranjane with their lives if necessary.

"The First and Second Ravna Gora troops are charged with guarding the plateau. They will have approximately ten thousand troops distributed throughout the villages within a fifteen mile radius of the airfield." Mihailovich paused for a moment as the men absorbed the information.

"They will block all the roads and paths leading here, even the cow paths. In addition, they will enforce a total ban on movement to and from here. This will ensure that the Germans will not be anywhere near the field. As an added precaution, we will have two thousand of our best armed men spread around the immediate vicinity of the airstrip."

The magnitude of the number of troops that he could rally in such a short time was staggering to O'Donnell. And that they would risk their own lives to ensure that no American life would be lost in this mission amazed him. He knew that the Chetniks were committed to the Allied cause, but it never ceased to amaze him how committed the Serbs were to the Americans.

"That's good to hear, General Mihailovic," replied O'Donnell. "That should provide enough ground protection in the event we are discovered." He turned his attention to Musulin. "How are we going to get this many people out without being discovered?"

"We have looked at all the evacuation possibilities. We've determined that the evacuation has to be a night operation. That will provide us the initial cover from the enemy. But because of the extremely hazardous conditions and limited night visibility, we will have to keep the number of rescued airmen per C-47 at a minimum. We are looking at roughly twelve men per plane."

"Twelve men? We would need over twenty flights just to get everyone out of here," said one of the council members.

"That gives the Nazis twenty chances to shoot us down and kill us," said another.

"We need to keep the load on the planes as light as possible. So in addition to keeping the number of soldiers to a minimum, the planes will not carry any additional equipment or armaments. And the fuel supply will be kept to the absolute minimum as well. That means each mission will have to be flown with extreme precision and accuracy. Otherwise, they will run out of gas before they make it back to Italy."

The council agreed that although the plan was not ideal it was their only hope. O'Donnell was skeptical, but he understood the necessary precautions that had to be placed to increase the chances of success.

"The airmen will be divided into six groups of forty to fifty men. Each group will be housed in a different nearby village and under the command of its own officer. This should minimize the danger in case the Germans discover us and stage a surprise attack," Musulin continued. "Each group will have a predetermined time of arrival to the airfield."

The council ironed out some of the last minute details and prepared to disperse. Musulin stopped them before they left.

"We need everyone's help and the grace of God for this to work. I know you are all up for the challenge. It's time to go home boys."

As preparations for the upcoming evacuation continued, O'Donnell saw General Mihailovic and his interpreter walking through camp. He had just finished speaking with Musulin, Jibilian and Rajacich. Compelled to have a few words alone with him, O'Donnell ran up to the General.

"Excuse me General Mihailovic," shouted O'Donnell as he approached them.

General Mihailovic stopped and turned to face O'Donnell. He smiled at the young soldier. "Yes?"

Not sure of what he was going to say, O'Donnell decided it was best to speak from his heart. "General Mihailovic, sir, I hope I can have a few minutes of your time."

"You may. Let's sit beneath that tree. I could use a short rest," the general replied with a grin.

They sat under the tall tree. It was hot and humid, but the shade, combined with the slight breeze, offered some relief from the heat. O'Donnell wiped the sweat from his forehead.

"General, I want to thank you and your men, and your people for all that has been done for me and the other soldiers. You have all done everything you could to ensure our safety. I don't even know if the words thank you are sufficient."

"You're welcome. But this is what we do. We do not abandon our allies, even if they have abandoned us," he replied

"I am not really sure how that all happened," O'Donnell replied, "but I see now that it is a mistake."

"Yes, the Allies have made a mistake. And unfortunately, our people are suffering because of it. But, we believe that the Americans will see the error they have made and return their support to us."

"Why are you helping us?"

"You are young, maybe that is why it is difficult for you to understand. We are a small nation of hardworking, honest people. All we have ever wanted was to live our lives in the kind of freedom that Americans have. Unfortunately, we have always had to fight for it. And pay for it with our blood.

"For thousands of years, we have had one enemy or another invade and attack us. And each time, we battled our way to freedom. We may not have much in the way of material riches, but we have our Serbian Orthodox faith, identity, families, honor and pride. For most of us, that is the highest form of wealth."

He paused as he took off is hat and ran his fingers through his hair. Wiping his own forehead, he said, "Is this how the weather is in America?"

"Summer is summer. We have it pretty much the same back home," laughed O'Donnell.

"We are more similar than we are different. Language is our greatest barrier," commented the General.

"General, you know that at this point, the Allies still think you are collaborating with the Nazis. I am not sure if that is going to change, even with this evacuation.

"But I think the evacuation might get them to allow for your safety to be taken into consideration. If we defeat the Germans, Tito will do everything in his power to take credit for it. And then your safety will be in jeopardy. I will talk to Musulin to see if we can arrange for you to be evacuated along with us. It could be your only chance for survival."

Mihailovic shook his head. He looked thoughtfully towards the sky as he formulated his thoughts. Looking at O'Donnell, he spoke quietly.

"I appreciate your offer, very much. And it humbles me to think you value my life so. However, I must refuse. I am a Serb, loyal to the Serbian people. My place, dead or alive, is with them."

CHAPTER 17

August 9, 1944

DAYS OF FOCUSED preparation for the rescue evacuation had passed. They were putting on the finishing touches and prepared to wait for this evening's arrival of the C-47s.

O'Donnell, Musulin, Jibilian, Rajacich and a hundred others took a short break to relax as sheep and cows grazed nearby. The animals mewed quietly as the warm summer breeze bristled the leaves of the nearby trees. The airstrip looked about as good as it was going to get. They had leveled it as much as possible and extended its length to provide a relatively safe landing for the planes.

But even with all of the preparations, it was still a field that was, just six days ago, used to graze animals.

O'Donnell lay on his back, with a blade of grass between he teeth. He closed his eyes and thought of his conversation with General Mihailovic. His impression of the man never faltered.

It was easy to see why the Serbian people adored him.

He sat up and watched as the Chetniks and airmen shared their last moments with each other. Over the course of their stay with the Serbian Chetniks, the airmen formed close relationships and bonds with them.

Groups of men gathered around the field, some laughing as they reminisced about their adventures together. Others cried openly, knowing that this was probably the last time they would see each other. O'Donnell watched Wallace hug Branko as tears streamed down his face.

There would be little time tonight for farewells. Time was pinpoint precise for success. So they were taking advantage of this short time to say their farewells.

O'Donnell laughed as he saw several airmen take off their shoes and pieces of clothing and give them to the peasants and Chetniks. Shoes and good clothes were in critical supply. With harsh winter conditions just around the corner, the Americans thought there was not better gift they could give their new friends than a warm pair of shoes that would prevent frostbite.

The Serbs gave gifts in return. They handed them small trinkets for the airmen to remember them by. It was a heartwarming sight for O'Donnell. This was true good human nature.

The farewells continued as O'Donnell and others rested lazily near the airfield. O'Donnell was slowly drifting off to sleep when he heard the buzzing sound of engines in the distance.

He sat up quickly and looked out towards the sound. Everyone else heard the planes and scattered toward the tree line. O'Donnell hid the sun from his eyes and focused on the planes.

They were flying low, about one thousand feet above ground. He immediately recognized them as three German Stuka dive-bombers. And they were flying directly over the airfield.

"Cover!" O'Donnell shouted as they all scrambled to hide in surrounding bushes and trees.

"They'll see the airfield! It's over! All for nothing!" shouted one of the soldiers.

O'Donnell's heart sank as the planes neared. If they saw the airstrip, they would definitely report it and the Nazis would attack immediately. His hopes plummeted. All this time, they'd been able to hide everything from the Nazis. Now, just hours away from rescue, they were about to be discovered.

He closed his eyes and prayed that somehow, someway, God would prevent them from seeing the airfield. When he opened his eyes, he was shocked.

The cows and sheep that were grazing nearby had moved from those grassy fields to the airfield. They were spread out across the entire area, like they were trying to hide the area from the bombers!

The planes flew overhead and everyone was immobilized, afraid that breathing alone would give them away to the Germans. The planes passed the airfield and continued flying towards their destination.

"Do you think the cows covered it well enough?" Wallace asked as he walked up to O'Donnell.

"I don't know. It's hard to tell from this viewpoint. And it's too late to warn Bari, pick up is only hours away, replied O'Donnell. "I said a prayer as they approached us. I guess you can say it was answered."

"I hope you're right, O'Donnell."

As a precaution, Mihailovich sent his troops to check on the German garrisons that surrounded Pranjane. They looked for any sign of increased activity that indicated that the airfield had been discovered.

When they returned, they reported nothing out of the ordinary. From the looks of things, the Germans had been fooled again. How long could their luck hold out?

At nightfall, the prearranged groups assembled at the airstrip.

Tensions were high as they anxiously awaited the arrival of the rescue planes. At precisely ten o'clock they heard the engines.

The ground crew flashed the signal. They blinked three dashes "Oscar". The plane responded with "kilo." They scrambled and lit the fire pots.

The wind had been shifting all day. O'Donnell hoped it wouldn't shift towards the trees. If it did, a landing would be impossible.

"Hold on, wind. Just hold on. Don't disappoint us now," O'Donnell whispered as he watched the first plane approach. It began its slow descent towards the runway.

"It's going too fast. They are going to overshoot the field," said a pilot standing near O'Donnell.

They watched as the plane flew over the field and continued on.

"No!" hissed O'Donnell. "Come on! Not after all of this!"

The second and third planes also misjudged the strip. Hope quickly plummeted. The fourth plane approached quickly. Everyone held their breath and hoped for a landing.

The plane began its descent sooner and approached the ground. It bounced a few times before it landed then raced towards the edge of the plateau! The pilot braked as hard as he could while the others watched in horror as the plane raced forward.

The plane screeched to a halt just inches from the edge.

"Woohoo!" shouted the men.

"Yea!" others shouted and shot their fists into the air.

The first twelve airmen raced for the plane, hopping and scrambling to take off their shoes and jackets. They jumped into the plane and threw their shoes and jackets to the celebrating Serbs, who shouted out their thanks and goodbyes as the plane immediately took off. It retracted its wheels just in time to avoid hitting the trees as it ascended into the night sky.

"Son of a gun!" shouted O'Donnell! "We did it!" He laughed as he slapped Wallace on the back.

"Still got a lot of men to get out of here, but, yea, we did it," said Wallace.

They watched as the fifth plane overshot the airstrip and gunned around. It tried again, this time with a slow descent towards a landing. It landed and taxied around.

The plane slowed to a near stop when its wheel got stuck near a ditch. The plane teetered towards the ditch. Everyone jumped and raced to stop it from falling in. They surrounded the side of the plane and pushed several times until they moved it out of the ditch and back onto the strip.

The next twelve airmen repeated the earlier scene and boarded the plane. As it flew away, their Serbian hosts waved their goodbyes and blew kisses to the Americans. They celebrated another successful takeoff.

Musulin thought about the three planes that didn't make it, and the other two that nearly didn't.

"It's too dangerous. We're pushing our luck." Rajacich and Jibilian agreed.

"We can't allow any more planes to land on these conditions. Night rescue is too dangerous, especially with a makeshift airstrip on a damn plateau.

"Block off the strip and signal the planes to return to base without landing." Musulin commanded.

Disappointed, the remaining airmen did as they were told. For now, they were still stuck in Yugoslavia. But they had no intentions of leaving the airstrip, so they remained there the rest of the evening.

Musulin radioed headquarters and informed them of the situation.

"Standby for further instructions," was their reply.

Early the following morning, O'Donnell and the others were

awakened by an earsplitting noise in the distance. They quickly rose and looked up into the sky to see what was causing the incredible noise.

"Holy Mother of God!" exclaimed Wallace.

"Are you kidding me?" shouted O'Donnell.

The sky was saturated with American airplanes! O'Donnell counted six C-47s surrounded by at least one hundred P-51 and P-38 fighter planes! Amazing!

"This is headquarters' answer!" laughed Musulin.

Everyone erupted in cheers as it dawned on them that today was the day! Evidently, headquarters decided that the only safe rescue could be one done during the day under the protection of fighter planes.

Daytime conditions changed the parameters of the rescue. Word quickly spread that now the planes could accommodate twenty airmen instead of twelve. This meant fewer planes to complete the rescue. O'Donnell was in awe at the magnitude of the rescue.

The fighter planes flew a fifty-mile radius around Pranjane. Every German supply convoy, freight train and troop encampment within that radius was destroyed.

The American fighter planes continued their attack on the surrounding Germans. Hundreds of bombs dropped and thousands of bullets and missiles were shot. The impact of surrounding explosions combined with the roar of the engines of the rescuing C-47's was intense.

"It's amazing. One of the greatest airshows of this war," thought O'Donnell with pride. "This is what I'm talking about! America!" he whooped as he jumped in the air.

O'Donnell laughed as he ran towards the planes. Wallace was getting ready to board. O'Donnell would be one of the last ones, but he wanted to say his goodbyes.

"Wallace, be safe! See you in Italy!" he shouted.

Wallace saluted O'Donnell before climbing aboard the plane. Within minutes O'Donnell watched as Wallace's plane took off.

Thirty minutes later another group of six c-47s arrived under the same cover of fighter planes. One hundred and twenty airmen boarded the planes and were now on their way back to Italy.

O'Donnell waited for the last set of planes. Branko walked up to him and shook his hand.

"Thank you. Friend," he said to O'Donnell as he handed him a black towel folded into a small square. Confused, O'Donnell unfolded the towel. It wasn't a towel at all. He was looking at a black flag with a white skull and cross bones in the center with the words "Sloboda ili Smrt, za Kralja I Otadjbina". The Chetnik flag and he knew it translated to "Freedom or Death. For the King and our Fatherland." Touched, O'Donnell shook his hand.

"No, thank you. You are one young brave soldier. And I am proud to have been on a mission with you." O'Donnell didn't know if Branko fully understood what he told him. But he wanted to say it anyway.

O'Donnell, with his coat over his arm, looked over his shoulders as the last group of planes that landed. He quickly unbuttoned his shirt and took it off. He slipped off his shoes and socks and put them in his coat along with this shirt and handed it all to Branko.

"Take these. It can't nearly repay what you've all done for the others and me. But it is a start. Stay Chetnik strong, Branko."

O'Donnell jogged to the plane and boarded with the others.

He sat among this last group of airmen, Chetnik flag on his lap and looked out the window. He saw General Mihailovic in the distance watching as the final planes of the day taxied to takeoff.

When he thought he had caught the General's eye, O'Donnell

saluted him, honored to have met such a remarkable man. The General saw him, stood straight and saluted him in return.

O'Donnell watched as Pranjane and his Chetnik saviors disappeared through the clouds.

CHAPTER 18

ETROVICH WATCHED WITH joy as wave after wave of C-47s landed, bringing with them hundreds of rescued airmen. He anxiously scanned each group of men as they departed their planes, looking for O'Donnell's face among them.

But as each group dispersed, his hopes that O'Donnell would be one of them diminished. He knew that it was a long shot, but he continued to hope that O'Donnell would be alive and well.

The last group of planes arrived from Yugoslavia. Petrovich waited impatiently to see if O'Donnell would be among this last group. It was his last hope.

One after another, the airmen exited the planes. O'Donnell was not one of them. In mourning, he bowed his head to offer an overdue silent prayer for his friend's soul.

"Is that anyway to welcome home a friend? By daydreaming in the middle of the base?" asked O'Donnell as he stood in front Petrovich.

Petrovich opened his eyes and saw a dirty, shoeless, sockless and shirtless O'Donnell standing in front of him.

"What did they do to your clothes?" laughed Petrovich.

"It's a long story. I'll tell you all about it, after a long shower!"

In the end, two hundred and forty-three Americans and

twenty Russians, French Canadians and British were rescued from Pranjane within those two days of the evacuation. Over the course of the next several weeks, many more batches of rescued airmen arrived in Pranjane to be arranged for evacuation.

In thanks, Mihailovic and his Chetnik army received one and a half tons of medical supplies - barely enough to fill half of an aircraft. And certain British and Americans in Bari, Red included, were vehemently opposed to even that meager amount of aid.

Later, O'Donnell learned that as the planes were coming to Chetnik territory to rescue the airmen, they were also dropping off supplies to Tito and his Partisan army. He couldn't believe the audacity and betrayal. Mihailovic, his men and the Serbian peasants had risked it all to save Americans, and we were dropping off supplies and medicine to his enemy. And that enemy was surely going to use those supplies against Mihailovich.

To make matters even worse, O'Donnell and the others were ordered not to share their story with anyone. The military authorities classified the mission as top secret and they were forbidden from disclosing any details.

"I don't understand. They rescued us. Why should that be a secret?" argued O'Donnell. "In fact, it was an amazing rescue. People have a right to know!"

"That is an order. You and the others will not share your experience in the Mihailovic camp and you will not disclose the events of the mission. If you do, you will be violating direct orders and as such you will be punished accordingly," replied O'Donnell's commanding officer.

To the airmen's complete surprise, the position of the British and Americans hadn't changed. They still viewed Tito as their ally. O'Donnell and the others were forced to listen to briefings on Yugoslavia that described Mihailovic and his Chetniks as the enemy. O'Donnell and the others could barely contain themselves, short of being court martialed for disobeying orders

"The enemy?" questioned O'Donnell. "They aren't the enemy. I wouldn't be here if it wasn't for the Chetniks!"

"That's enough, O'Donnell," reprimanded his commanding officer. "As I have told you before, you are not to tell anyone what happened in Yugoslavia. NO ONE. Do you understand me? This is a direct order!"

"Yes sir. I do understand you. But it's not right. Not right at all."

Red continued his opposition to General Mihailovich and continued his support of Tito. O'Donnell and Petrovich confronted him one evening. O'Donnell twirled between his fingers the red star Petrovich had found months earlier.

"Hey, Red. I think you lost something," said O'Donnell as he tossed the star to Red.

"Wherever did you find this?" Red smiled. "Perhaps from your stint in Yugoslavia? What a wonderful gift. Thank you!" he said with a sneer.

*　　*　　*

On December 27, 1944, the final evacuation took place. Musulin was replaced two weeks after the successful completion of the main evacuation in August. Nick Lalich, who was among those on the very first set of cargo planes to touch down in Pranjane, took over for him.

In all, over five hundred Allied men were rescued with the help of General Draza Mihailovich and his Chetniks in the greatest rescue mission of World War II.

O'Donnell contemplated this as he crouched down in front of his bed and pulled out a small worn box. He slowly opened it and looked inside. On top of the other items was the black

Chetnik flag Branko had given him. He took it out of the box. Taking his time, he unfolded it and spread it out on his bed.

He traced the skull and cross bones with his finger and remembered a remarkable General and his people, who risked everything to save him and those other five hundred men. The guilt that plagued him was unbearable. How could he ever repay them if he couldn't even talk about what they did?

"I swear I will spend the rest of my life trying to find a way to let the world know what you did for us. Every waking moment, whenever possible, I will thank you for giving me my life back. And I will do what I can to give you the thanks and respect you deserve."

Tears streaming down his face, O'Donnell folded the flag, carefully placed it back in the box, and slid it under his bed.

EPILOGUE

I N 1945, THE Germans were defeated and forced to leave occupied countries, including Yugoslavia. Tito took control of Yugoslavia and established a communist state that deprived the people of Yugoslavia the freedoms that they so desperately fought for, during World War I, World War II and every war over the course of their existence.

Although it was never publicly admitted, it has been said that Churchill and Roosevelt privately acknowledged that they had made a mistake supporting Tito and abandoning Mihailovich. Eventually, the truth about the moles that had infiltrated their commands and manipulated information in favor of Tito emerged. Unfortunately, both for Mihailovich and the people of Yugoslavia, it was too late.

Obsessed, Tito engaged in a campaign to capture Mihailovich. The Chetniks were forced to leave Yugoslavia and seek refuge in other countries, with many emigrating to the United States. Most had to leave their wives and children behind, leaving them in the unmerciful hands of the Communists. As they were forced to leave the country, thousands of other Chetniks were killed by both the Partisans and Croatian Ustasha.

Mihailovich, ill with typhus, evaded the Partisans with the

help of his dedicated Chetnik soldiers who carried him on stretchers from village to village. Friends urged him to leave Yugoslavia to save his life but he refused.

On March 25, 1946, American newspapers announced that Mihailovich had been captured and was to be tried as a Nazi collaborator and enemy of the state. American airmen all across the United States rallied to save the man who had risked so much for them.

They wrote their senators and congressmen, pleading for an intervention at the trial. The American airmen knew Tito's tactics and they were convinced that the trial would be a farce. If you were against Tito, you were considered an enemy and guilty, regardless of the evidence to the contrary.

They appealed to Tito's court, asking to be witnesses for Mihailovic, to prove the accusations of Nazi collaboration to be false. They were denied. Carrying signs that read, "Tito's court said Mihailovich killed me," they demonstrated in major cities across the United States, especially in Washington DC, demanding to be heard. Desperate to save Mihailovich, they also wrote newspapers and contacted radio stations.

Tito and his court denied them again. In a typical tactic, Mihailovic was drugged to prevent him from defending himself. Tito's prosecutors presented false documents and information, and claimed that the Partisans were the ones who rescued the American airmen, not Mihailovic.

On June 10, 1946, as expected, and to the extreme disappointment of the rescued Airmen, Tito's mock court found Mihailovich guilty of war collaboration and treason. Throughout his trial, the communist courtroom spectators hissed and taunted. Despite their overt hostility, Mihailovic closed his defense in a calm and dignified manner. Although he was tired, battered and drugged, Mihailovich stood before his condemners and spoke his last public words.

"During the first World War, I was wounded and received medals for valor. I stayed at the front all the time when I could have left. I never used brutality to the enemy, much less to my own people.

When war came and our front broke, I was left with a broken-spirited people and with a legacy of the rottenness of two decades. I went into the forest and told the people to hide their weapons. I wanted to continue resistance, and thus I became a rebel against Hitler's Germany.

At that time, only England and I were still at war.

I proclaimed that my army would be a Yugoslav Army. Others wished to have only a Serbian Army, but I proved to them the greatness of Yugoslavia as an idea. Unfortunately, some other commanders would not accept this.

Partisans appeared immediately when Soviet Russia entered the war. The Germans began to take reprisals, and some of the people begged me not to emerge. My first success was when ten Partisan plunderers came over to me. I had an action against those Partisans, who, peasant women told me had been pillaging. I released them and warned them not to behave in that manner any more . . .

I had three meetings with Marshal Tito, to which I went sincerely. I told him I believed we could come to an understanding, and that both sides had made mistakes. Unfortunately, we spent our time in mutual accusations. Obviously, even before I met him, our battle had already begun . . .

I deny that I had ever handed over Partisan prisoners to the Germans. The blame lies entirely on the witness who testified against me. He was in fact the collaborator.

German reprisals had been terrible. I'd seen flames burning villages. My 5,000 men were not anything against five German divisions. I told the London Government but go no instructions in return. So I went with two other men to the Germans. We took grenades in case of treachery from them.

The Germans would not parley. They called for our unconditional surrender and I was called a rebel. I was astonished and said I was fighting for my country and they must, as soldiers, understand this. I refused to drink wine with the Germans and there was NO agreement. I told the Germans I would fight. Soon after, they attacked my headquarters in Ravna Gora and killed many of my men.

I deny that I had ever had a representative at Italian headquarters.

I had never ordered action against civilians and could never even approve it. I could never favor killing a man without a trial.

I remind the court of Hitler's message to Mussolini, saying that I was the greatest enemy of the Axis and that I was only waiting for the right moment to attack.

My other meeting with the Germans was conducted with the American Colonel McDowell. That meeting was to negotiate a surrender of German arms and not for collaboration.

I wanted nothing for myself.

I never wanted the old Yugoslavia, but I had a difficult legacy.

I am a soldier who sought to organize resistance to the Axis for our own country and for the rising of all of the Balkan peninsula.

I am sorry that anyone should think I have been disloyal to the Government. I was caught in a whirlpool of events and the movements of the new Slav unity, which I have favored for a long time.

I had against me a competitive organization, the

Communist Party, which seeks its aims without compromise. I was faced with changes in my own Government, and accused of connections with every possible secret service, enemy and Allied.

I believed I was on the right road and called for any foreign journalist or Red Army Mission to visit me and see everything. But fate was merciless to me when it threw me into this maelstrom.

I strove for much. I undertook much. But the gales of the world have carried away both me and my work.

I ask the court to judge what I have said according to its proper value."

—The Times, July 12, 1946. The Daily Telegraph and
Morning Post, July 12, 1946.

He spoke for over four and a half hours, and at his conclusion, the entire courtroom was overcome with silence. The correspondents representing London newspapers: The Times, The Daily Telegraph and Morning Post were impressed with his words and evidently, so was the communist audience. Though his defense was solid and impactful, it was to no avail. Tito's government had never intended on Mihailovic being a free man again.

On July 17, 1946, General Draza Mihailovich, World War II's greatest guerilla general and friend to the United States and Allies, was executed by a Communist firing squad and buried in an unmarked grave.

Across the United States, grown men wept at the news. They would spend the rest of their lives defending Mihailovic and the Chetniks.

AUTHORS NOTE

THIS STORY IS historical fiction. While several characters and situations are fictionalized, it is based on true events, the most important one being the actual rescue mission. The story is a compilation of stories gathered from the rescued airmen and the members of the Air Rescue Unit Team.

Musulin, Jibilian, Rajacich, Lalich, and Mihailovich are real people. The other characters were created out of a combination of the stories of several airmen and people of Yugoslavia. These men, along with Major Richard Felman, on whom much of O'Donnell's character is based, spent the rest of their lives fighting to clear the names of Mihailovic, the Chetniks and the Serbian people.

General Eisenhower, President of the United States of America in 1953, was instrumental in seeing that Mihailovic was honored by the United States. He was one of many who convinced President Truman to posthumously award Draza Mihailovich the highest award possible for a foreign nationalist: the Legion of Merit. It was awarded for rescuing the airmen and for his overall effort in the war, proving he was not collaborating with the enemy. Unfortunately, the award was not made public.

Airmen tried to erect a monument in Washington DC to honor General Draza Mihailovic and to commemorate the

Halyard Mission. But the United States government worried it would offend Tito, who ruled Yugoslavia with an iron fist until his death in 1980 and who spent his entire life demonizing Mihailovic and the Chetniks with propaganda and lies. The monument was never erected.

Yugoslavia broke apart in the late 1980s with the support of countries such as Germany, Great Britain and the United States. For most of the 1990's the country was entrenched in one of the bloodiest civil wars since World War II.

Much of the deep-rooted hatred was seeded during World War II and from the atrocities committed by the Croatian and Muslim Ustasha and the German Nazis. The media inaccurately portrayed the recent war as a war of aggression, comparing it to Nazi Germany of World War II, instead of what it really was: a civil war.

The inaccurate portrayal and blatant anti-Serbian propaganda perpetrated by the countries that supported the breakup of Yugoslavia, once again turned celebrated allies of America into modern day monsters.

The airmen watched in horror as the Serbian people were once again betrayed by the Americans, as NATO bombs fell on Belgrade and Serbia for seventy-two days straight, as Serbians were stripped of their rights in Croatia, Bosnia and Kosovo, and as hundreds of thousands of Serbians were forced from their ancestral homes under the supervision of an American led NATO mission.

The airmen continued to tell their story throughout the civil war, in hopes that people would see through the propaganda and to the truth. In the end, communism fell and the truth about Mihailovic slowly emerged. Annually, various Congressmen, at the requests of the airmen and their families, continue to call for recognition of what Mihailovich and his Chetniks did for the United States.

In 1997, the British declassified information related to the Halyard Mission. Within those documents, it was confirmed that communist moles that infiltrated the British SOE did indeed play significant roles in the British decision to switch support from Mihailovich to Tito. The communist deceit was finally revealed.

On May 9, 2005, George Vujnovich, Arthur Jibilian, Clare Musgrove and a few other rescued airmen presented the Legion of Merit to Mihailovich's daughter, Gordana. It was finally where it belonged, in the hands of a Mihailovich.

May the memory of all of the rescued airmen, the Air Rescue Unit, their Chetnik friends and General Draza Mihailovich be eternal. And may their sacrifices and bravery never be forgotten.

For more information of the Halyard Mission, please read:

The Forgotten 500: The Untold Story of the Men Who Risked All for the Greatest Rescue Mission of World War II. Freeman, Gregory A., (2008) Penguin.

The Web of Disinformation-Churchill's Yugoslav Blunder, Martin, David (1990), Harcourt Brace Jovanovic, New York, NY

Mihailovic and I. Felman, Richard, L. (1964)

Nikola Tesla Society http://www.teslasociety.com/jibilian_remembered.htm

A special thank you to Father Dragomir Tuba and St. Sava Serbian Orthodox Church, Phoenix, AZ for allowing access to The Major Richard Felman Operation Halyard Collection, from the library of St. Sava Serbian Orthodox Church.